YAR/T

7Days

For Dad. Always.

First published in the UK in 2015 by Scholastic Children's Books
An imprint of Scholastic Ltd
Euston House, 24 Eversholt Street
London, NW1 1DB, UK

Registered office: Westfield Road, Southam, Warwickshire, CV47 0RA
SCHOLASTIC and associated logos are trademarks and/
or registered trademarks of Scholastic Inc.

Text copyright © Eve Ainsworth, 2015

The right of Eve Ainsworth to be identified as the author
of this work has been asserted by her.

ISBN 978 1 407 14691 1

A CIP catalogue record for this book
is available from the British Library.

Printed and bound by CPI Group (UK) Ltd, Croydon, CR0 4YY
Papers used by Scholastic Children's Books
are made from wood grown in sustainable forests.

1 3 5 7 9 10 8 6 4 2

This is a work of fiction. Names, characters, places,
incidents and dialogues are products of the author's imagination
or are used fictitiously. Any resemblance to actual people,
living or dead, events or locales is entirely coincidental.

www.scholastic.co.uk

7 Days

Eve Ainsworth

SCHOLASTIC

If you're reading this I've succeeded. Good. I've done something right at last.

I've been thinking about it for ages, so don't go thinking it was a sudden decision. The only thing holding me back was the fact that I'm a pathetic coward. But, in the end I knew I could do it really. It's not so hard, not when you're at the end of the line. And I am now, believe me.

There's not much else I can write. Not to you anyway. Will you even read it?

You'll know why I did this. Everyone will know.

Sometimes in the darkness you begin to see so clearly. Because of this I now know that:

a) Bullies are scum.

b) Families should be there when you need them.

c) I am weak. I deserve this.

I hope this will end quickly. I hope it's like sleeping only without the rubbish dreams.

I hope you'll find her and tell her what I've done.

X

Kez Walker: Jesus, some people just don't care what they look like. Even outta school. . .

5 hours ago.

Like   Comment   Share

Lois: ??

Kez: LOL. Aw yeah – saw the STIG today . . . poor us. She actually hurt my eyes

Marnie: Who? Oh. I see – LOL. Yeah, we saw

Kez: Her hair! God. Does she wash?

Lois: ;o)

Marnie: Kez ur a legend mate!

Kez: Honestly tho, shes such a stig – and her shoes? Charity shop?

Marnie: Charity shop – def! She dresses like such a freak

Kez: Needs a lesson in style

Kez: Needs a lesson in sumthin anyway

Hannah: Not fair. Jess is all right.

Marnie: How did you know she was talking bout Jess?

Kez: Lol! How many other stigs do you know?

Hannah: I'm just saying, shes OK

Kez: Yeah well – u would say that. Ur her little pal

Marnie: So funny

Kez: Don't matter - Stig will get it. She's doing my head in. She offends my eyes

Lois: 4 real? When

Kez: Soon. . .

Monday

You poor little cow. She offends my eyes. Big mistake. On your knees and say it. This is not over. Please, please, please. You better show your face. RIP. Have you looked in the mirror lately? There's nothing to worry. RIP. Fat. This is not over. We need to talk. LOL. Evil. Gross. LOL. Fat. Does she wash? Evil. Does she wash? Evil. This is not over. We need to talk. LOL. Fat. Poor little cow. You needed to LOL. Please, please, be taught a lesson. please. Evil. Gross. lesson. It's fine, honest. You're pathetic. Fat. worry about the police. On your knees and say it. There's nothing to Next time I'm calling the police. say it. Gross and Fat. Fat. RIP. Evil. you fat little freak. Big mistake. Gross. You needed to be taught a lesson. It'll just make things worse. Have you looked in the mirror lately? It's fine, honest. RIP. We need to talk. Gross. LOL. Yeah, whatever. She dresses like such a freak.

Jess

I don't need an alarm clock any more. Good job really, because Hollie spilt juice on my old glitter fairy one. Now the digital screen has a permanent blurry black mark on it, like a bruise. No matter how many times I rub it with wet wipes, it still feels sticky under my fingers. I won't throw it away though. Dad bought it for me four years ago. His fingerprints must still be on the plastic, so that's part of him that's with me – damaged or not. It sits beside my bed, next to my glass of water, flashing its broken time like a lighthouse in the fog.

I don't need an alarm clock any more, because I have my own way of waking up – a crippling, unbearable feeling of sickness. It's the same every morning. My eyelids open and then my body registers where I am. My stomach twists and turns, my legs feel like jelly and my throat begins to tighten. Every part of me, every fibre, nerve and muscle is fighting the feeling of dread, the realization that I have to face another day.

Today is no different.

I swing my legs out of the bed, large lumps of meat that wobble as I move. I hate the way they dimple. I hate their look – chicken flesh, pumped fat ready to burst. I pull my T-shirt down, trying to hide the roll of skin that skims over my knickers, and ease myself up.

The room is a mess, which annoys me. Hollie is useless at tidying; leaving trails of destruction everywhere – dolls, books, funny plastic monsters with strange faces. I have to tread carefully to make sure I don't step on something. I kick one troll-like figure across the room and watch as it bounces against my bookcase. It lands on its head with its weird beady eyes glaring at me.

"You can get lost," I tell it. It just stares back, grinning.

Hollie sleeps on the small bed under the window and, as usual, her body is sprawled in the weirdest position – her legs hanging off the mattress and her arms bent up behind her head. She looks odd. Her mouth hangs open and strands of hair are stuck to her face in damp stripes. One eye is half open. I wonder what she's dreaming about.

"Hollie." I shake her gently, waiting as she groans and then rolls into a ball. "Come on, sleepy. School."

"Nooooo. Ten more minutes," she says, pulling the duvet blindly, kicking me at the same time.

"Sorry. No time. Come on, wash and uniform."

I look around the room but Mum's not left anything out. I pick up the puddle of clothes beside Hollie's bed, left from last night. I inspect them for dirt, but they look OK apart from a splodge of paint on her jumper which I pick off with my fingernail. Her tights are getting a bit small, so I pull on them to stretch them out. It feels like a weird exercise.

"My top's got a hole in it," Hollie says, getting up slowly. "Jack said it looked stupid yesterday."

"Tell him he's stupid."

Hollie grins at me, gappy toothed, her blonde hair still stuck against her face. "You're funny."

I take her hand and lead her into the bathroom, trying to ignore the reflection in the mirror as I walk past.

"Yeah, I'm funny," I say.

But not in the way she thinks.

*

I am pouring the last of the Rice Krispies into our bowls when Mum walks through the front door. It's raining and her hair is pressed against her face in a matted lump. Her face is red and shiny and droplets of water are still dripping off the end of her nose. She needs a new umbrella. I remember the last one blew inside-out on the way to the shops. She battled with it for ages, before swearing and dumping it in a nearby hedge.

I wonder if it's still there.

"Is there milk left for me?" she says, shaking her mac and dumping her bag in the corner of the kitchen. Her eyes are dark and hooded, like she could just sleep right there, standing up. I can't look at her for long; the worry claws at me too much. I can't even remember the last time she smiled.

"There's some," I say. I was hoping to have a small glass myself but it doesn't matter, she obviously needs it more. I flick on the kettle and look around for a clean mug. The sink is piled high with dirty dishes. I really don't want to put my hand in the slimy cold water that is pooling in the plates from last night. Instead I find a chipped "I love England" cup by the breadbin and throw a teabag in. I see the packet of biscuits still rolled up behind the old bread. I twist the packet open and shove two chocolate digestives into my mouth. They are stale and sweet between my teeth. I see Mum staring at me, her eyes narrowed in disappointment.

"That was a full packet yesterday," she says.

I turn away, my face burning.

"Are you very tired, Mummy?" asks Hollie, eating her bowl of cereal while staring at Mum, wide-eyed.

"Yes," Mum says. She sits gingerly on the chair opposite; as if her bones are really heavy. She kicks off her shoes and stretches out her feet. She's wearing tights and the ends are dark with wet. She sighs. "It was a tough few hours."

Mum usually slips out just after we've gone to bed. Most nights she's back home after a few hours, but this week she's working double shifts because one of the other cleaners is off sick. The number for where she works is pinned on the fridge, just in case. I don't tell her that the worry of something actually happening leaves me hollow with panicked thoughts. The pinned-up number and the muttered words "just in case" only increase the feelings.

"Why don't you sleep when we do?" Hollie

asks as she prods the little Krispies with her spoon, making them dance.

"You know why." Her answers are blunt, sharp blasts. She is looking at the wall. "I have to work. Cleaning's all I can get. I'll sleep when you're gone."

She won't though. I know this because I've come home before and found her on the internet – tapping away on her different forums. When we come home, that's often where we'll find her. She can't talk to me, but thousands of invisible cyber-people know what she's thinking. To me she's like a treasure chest, securely locked away and heavily guarded. I just wish I knew what she wasn't saying.

I give her the tea and then sit down with my dry cereal. I don't have as much as Hollie. Mine are mainly broken bits from the bottom. Hollie is happy though and is eating quickly, milk dribbling down her chin. All I can hear is her munching loudly and the ticking from the clock in the room next door.

"Hollie needs more clothes. You've not done the washing," I say.

"OK," she nods.

"Have we got washing powder?"

Her face squashes up. "I – oh, I don't know. Maybe.

Or not. I need to check." She rubs her temples, squashing up the skin.

"It's just — you've not done a shop for ages."

She turns then and finally looks at me, her eyes as bright as crystal. "That's because I have no money, Jessica."

Words are left unsaid, but I can still hear them. They hang in the air between us, so tangible I can almost reach out and touch them.

If you didn't keep eating everything, Jess. . .

She keeps staring at me, daring me to challenge her and of course I can't. She knows I won't.

I have so many words in my head, things that I want to tell Mum. I want to tell her all the bad thoughts that I keep trapped inside. I want to explain how hard it is being me.

But I look at her tired eyes again and my lips remain sealed.

It'll just be another week of the same.

Hollie and I walk to school together. It's not raining now and the sun is trying hard to push itself through the clouds. Hollie skips ahead. I shout at her to avoid the puddles; I'm not sure her shoes can take it. I walk carefully, trying to avoid the cracks in the pavement.

I remember Mum telling me that crocodiles would push their snouts through the gaps and snap at my toes. Silly, really, why did I ever believe her? How would they even fit for a start? And how could they survive under the paving slabs? So what if I'm fourteen, I still don't like to touch them – *just in case*, those words again. I guess it's because I believe something bad will happen to me if I even allow my foot to skim the edge.

Maybe today, if I can avoid the cracks, things will be different. Just one day, that's all I ask.

I hear her scream first and then I see Hollie lying flat on the ground. She must've tripped. She's like a baby in the middle of a temper tantrum, thumping the floor in rage. Her cries are loud and dramatic and I can see people on the street opposite looking over at us, eyebrows raised. An elderly lady with a large plastic shopping bag is standing facing me just inches away. She shakes her head and mutters something under her breath. As she moves past me she does a weird sideways jerk as if she's scared to touch me. I glare at her crumpled face, before racing over to my sister.

"Hollie, it's OK." I scoop her up in my arms. She is getting so big now and in her distress she's really hard to get hold of, thrashing against me and crying in pain. I struggle to pull her up, she feels too heavy. I keep whispering at her under my breath, trying to calm her, worried that I'm pulling her too hard. Finally, she relaxes and lets me move her towards me. I see the rip in her tights and the smear of blood on her knee. Hollie's eyes follow mine. Pure panic follows.

"I'm bleeding. I want to go home. I want Mummy."

I could imagine Mum's face if I were to take Hollie home now.

"Mum needs to rest, Hol – it's just a small cut, honest." I tap it gently with my finger. "See, magic dust will make it better. I have lots of it here!"

Hollie whimpers. "Not like Mummy. Mummy has more magic dust. Hers works better."

I can feel the eyes of the watchers burning into my back. Why are they so suspicious? Everyone on this estate seems to be like this lately; I feel judged everywhere I go. I don't want to be here too long, I can feel beads of sweat building and my armpits are damp. I need to move.

"C'mon. Let's get you to school. They have special plasters there."

I stand up and notice the dirt on my own trousers, which I try to brush off, but it only rubs it in even more. Hollie takes my hand and we start walking again, my sweaty palm clutching her small, sticky one. She is still whimpering, but quieter now. I have a nervous feeling in my stomach, like the blades of a blender going round and round. As we reach the main road, I know why it is. I'm scared someone from my school will see me, all sweaty and mucky. I look more revolting than ever. I know that I have limited time before crowds of them will appear. I have to move quickly.

I'm half dragging her now across the road, which is making her moan even more. "Stop pulling me. That hurts my hand. I want to go home. . ."

"Ssh, it's OK. We don't want to be late now, do we?"

Southwood Primary School is tucked down a small side road. There's barely any room to walk. We have to squeeze past the rows of cars that are parked there to get to the main entrance. The gate flaps uselessly, a group of boys kicked it in weeks ago and no one has bothered to fix it properly. I keep my head down, letting my hair fall in front of my face, the perfect veil.

The playground is like a large, empty lake, surprisingly cold-looking with no kids running around on it. We are late again. A few mums are walking out of the door, deep in conversation. They never notice us. Even back when Mum used to take Hollie, the other mums would keep away and stand in their own tight huddles. Mum used to call them the "playground panthers". She said she didn't mind, but I knew she wasn't being honest. She fiddled with her bottom lip when she said it. She always does that when she's lying.

I don't think Mum has any friends. Not any that I've met anyway.

Inside the school, it's warm and smells of paint. One of Hollie's bright pictures is on the wall staring at us when we walk in. I think it's meant to be a dog, but it has six legs.

Ms Matthews is waiting at the Year One doors. She smiles at us as we walk in – and then she notices Hollie's face.

"Oh dear. Why the tears?"

"She fell," I say, pointing at her tights. "Do you have a plaster?"

Ms Matthews smiles. She has a kind, podgy sort of face; it reminds me of a crumpet. She never asks too many questions and somehow she always understands what to do. "Of course. A pretty one? And I'm sure I can find some spare tights too."

Hollie's wide grin takes away a little of the panic inside of me. But as I kiss her tear-soaked cheek and glance up at the big red clock, my heart jumps in my chest.

Now I'm really late.

It's the worst thing, running into Perryfield High late. It's even worse when Kez, Lois and Marnie are there watching you do it.

I'm running in, sweating and panicking that Mr Ramon would be on patrol ready to dish out detentions for latecomers, and there they are – waiting by the main gate, cigarettes in their hands, smirks plastered across their smug faces.

I try to ease myself past them, attempting to look casual. Yeah, right. They just saw me sprinting up the road, trying to make my wobbly body go that little bit faster. Now I'm wheezing like an old woman and feeling sick, I couldn't look more stressed if I jumped into a vat of boiling water.

"Nice look," Kez says, a perfectly plucked eyebrow rising.

I ignore her and stagger past. I don't need this.

"Err, did the stig just touch you?"

I don't know who said that, probably Marnie. My stomach twists. I really don't want Kez on my case again – not now.

I turn slowly. Kez has moved closer and is facing me. She looks me up and down, a slow smile creeping up her face. I hate the fact that she is so beautiful. It's not fair. Her dark hair is worn high in a ponytail and has streaks of red in it. Her eyes are large and carefully made-up. They would be a beautiful blue, if they weren't so cold and hard.

"Haven't you got something to say to me?" she says softly, sweetly even.

I blink at her, confused. The sweat is still dripping down my back and I can feel my heart thumping in my chest. "I – I don't know what you mean. . ."

"You shoved past me. I think you should say something."

"I didn't," I say. "I didn't even touch you."

"Oh yes, you did." Marnie moves towards me. She is shorter with long blonde hair and downturned features. She reminds me of a dog. A dog caked in orange foundation. "You pushed past us with your sweaty, stiggy body."

"Err, gross," says Lois, who is standing further back, watching. Sometimes Lois is OK with me, but only sometimes. She's just as pretty as Kez but in a different way, more natural. She has beautiful red curls that tumble down her back in waves.

"I didn't touch you," I mumble, but the words are thick in my mouth. I can see Kez is mad now, her eyes are narrow and she's not smiling. I shouldn't have disagreed with her.

"You touched me, right!" she snarls, coming up close, "and I don't want you anywhere near me, understood?" She extends her finger and pushes me back, like I'm nothing. I hate it when she does that.

I nod anyway, looking down at my feet. I don't want to be here.

"Are you even listening to her?" Marnie yells. "You owe her an apology."

An apology? For what? Not touching her? When did life become so unfair? How come *she* can touch me with her stabbing fingernail?

"I'm sorry," I whisper.

"What?" says Kez, grinning again now, "I didn't quite hear that."

"I'm sorry. I'm sorry I touched you. I'm sorry I even dared to come near you."

"On your knees and say it," says Marnie.

I look at them, pleading. *Please don't make me do this.* Kez and Marnie keep smirking. Lois isn't looking; she's texting on her phone.

"Yeah, go on," says Kez, taking another drag of her cigarette, "in the dirt where you belong."

So I do it. I slowly bend down, on to the hard, cold concrete. Being lower than them is horrific. I feel like an animal or, even worse, an insect they could just squash with their shoe. Only inches away from me is an old lump of dog poo and a small trail of ants. The anger is burning in the back of my head, throbbing and threatening to burst out at any second. I concentrate hard on the ground because that way I don't have to see anyone walking past me. I don't need to know who is witnessing my humiliation.

"I'm sorry," I say again. "Now, please, let me go in. I'm so late."

I know I will get a detention now and I have to think about picking up Hollie. She gets so upset if I'm late.

"Let you go?" Kez laughs. "But that would mean you walking in with us. Like I said, Stig, I don't want you anywhere near me."

I don't reply. I concentrate instead on the small

line of ants making their way across the pavement in front of me, one of them is carrying a piece of yellow grain. The line is so perfect and in total unison.

"You can stay there until we're inside, get it?" Kez says.

"Yes."

"Good." She kicks my legs with her trainer. "And you really should think about losing some weight, sweetheart. Fat is never a good look, is it?"

No, it's not – I agree. They stride away, giggling among themselves – crushing my little ants under their feet as they go.

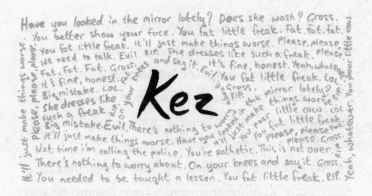

Have you looked in the mirror lately? Does she wash? Gross.
You better show your face. You fat little freak. Fat. Fat. Fat.
you fat little freak. It'll just make things worse. Please, please
we need to talk. Evil. RIP. She dresses like such a freak. Please
Fat. Fat. Fat. Gross. and say it. It's fine, honest. Yeah, whatev
it's fine, honest. Evil. You fat little freak. Lol
Big mistake. Lol. Gross. the mirror lately?
She dresses like little cow. Lol.
such a freak. It's fat little freak.
Big mistake. Evil. There's nothing to worr please, please fat
It'll just make things worse. Have you please. Gross.
Nxt time i'm calling the police. You're pathetic. This is not over.
There's nothing to worry about. On your knees and say it. Gross.
You needed to be taught a lesson. You fat little freak. RIP.

My phone is ringing again, buzzing gently on the bed beside me. I ignore it. Why doesn't she ever get the message? Maybe I should just answer and scream "la, la, la" at her. That would shut the stupid cow up. I've been awake for about an hour already and I feel like I've barely slept at all.

Marnie is sitting by her mirror, carefully inspecting her reflection. I think she's looking pretty rank actually; she's been wearing too much foundation lately — not that I'd dare tell her that. I watch as she smothers more on, a kind of orange glow coming from her face.

"Your mum?" she says, not turning around.

"Yeah." I reply, willing the screen to go blank. Finally it does and the room is silent again. I realize I've been holding my breath.

Marnie's room is in the biggest state ever; she actually keeps her entire wardrobe on the floor or stacked on her desk chair. When she shared it with her sister it used to be more organized, but since Jodie has moved away the whole place has pretty much exploded. At least Jodie's bed was clean; I'm not good with manky sheets. I always get an itchy, grossed-out feeling if I see a speck of dirt.

My mobile buzzes again. Mum just won't go away. She's obviously in that sort of mood. I open the text message reluctantly.

We need 2 talk. U can't keep stayin out all night.
Nxt time I'm callin the police.

Yeah, right, she wouldn't dare call them. Not unless she wants the social sniffing around.

"She's not happy," I tell Marnie, "silly cow. I told her I was staying here. She's probably forgotten and is freaking out."

Marnie shrugs. "She knows where you are. She's just stressing."

"It's not my fault she doesn't listen."

The phone buzzes again in my hand. If I didn't need it so much, I'd lob the stupid thing against the wall.

2night we're talkin. The 3 of us. Get it?

"Are you ready yet?" I bark at Marnie, stuffing my mobile into my bag. Mum can buzz me all she likes in there, I won't hear it. I'm certainly not going to answer her.

"I guess. I look so rough though," she moans, pulling down one of her eyes. "Look, it's all red. I'm gross. Crap! I hate Mondays!"

"You just need sleep. Talking about Ben all night was probably a bad idea."

Marnie sticks her tongue out at me and we both giggle. Across the hall I can hear the clatter of pans and the gushing of a tap being turned on.

"Mum's up then. Shall we grab some breakfast?"

I'm not hungry, but I get up to go with her. My body aches and my tongue is furry and fat in my mouth, like a giant moth. As I pass her mirror, I see my pale ghost-like face staring back and it surprises me. Huge dark bags ring my eyes and my skin looks as dry as tissue.

I'm looking more like her. Like Mum. I turn quickly away, hating the way that makes me feel.

Marnie lives in a block of flats right on the corner of the Macmillan "Mac" Estate. She's in Block B, a huge tower that is only overshadowed by its slightly darker cousin, Block A. Last night, we climbed up on to the roof. It was amazing just to see the entire town spread out beneath us like a giant kids' play mat. I could've stared for ages at the bright twinkling of the cars – tiny red dots moving away from this rat trap of a place. I don't hate the Estate; in fact it's probably my favourite area to be. I find it hard to describe why, but there is something free and honest about the Mac. No one is pretending to be what they're not; unlike the rest of this town. I honestly feel like I'm slowly suffocating at home. One day I'll get away. I always promise myself that.

One day.

Marnie likes living on the Mac. It's just her and her mum, Julie, and they get on pretty well. Julie is lovely. She works in the pub across the road and has a laugh that could wake half the street. She's so laid back, she's practically horizontal. She even turns a blind eye to Marnie smoking.

Julie throws a tenner at Marnie now, and kisses her on the cheek. "Get something nice for lunch," she says, all the time smiling in my direction.

It's weird but I kind of go awkward around Julie, as she sits there in her silk dressing gown, long bronzed legs spilling out. Marnie and her mum have such a good relationship, they're like mates really. I guess it's where Marnie gets her confidence from. Nothing fazes Marnie; I've never seen her upset or hurt – I swear she must be rock solid inside. That must be a good feeling.

"How's your mum, Kez?" Julie asks. She's not eating, just flicking through some magazine. She stops at a true-life story about some woman's arm getting trapped in a McDonald's drive-through. "My God, did you see this? She was only buying an Egg McMuffin – poor thing!"

"Er, gross," says Marnie, screwing up her face. "Do you have to show me that when I'm eating?"

"Sorry, darling." Julie throws the magazine on the floor. "People have such tragic lives, don't they? So how is your mum, Kez?"

Julie is smiling sweetly at me and I try not to let my hackles rise. She's not the type to wind people up. "She's fine," I say, sipping the orange juice that's been poured and trying to ignore the feeling of guilt that's building up inside me. I know Mum will be worrying, which isn't fair on her.

"And Dad? He's OK too, is he?"

I glance quickly at Marnie – has she said anything? But she just shrugs and carries on nibbling her toast. She has a lost look on her face and I know she must be thinking about Ben again.

27

"Yeah, fine," I reply. I know part of me is shutting down. I don't want to be questioned. I concentrate on picking my nails, hoping she'll get the message.

"Has he got a job yet? I know it's tough," she says, running her long, freshly polished fingernail over the rim of the cup. "He's in the pub an awful lot though, isn't he?"

I stand up. It's more dramatic than I mean it to be and the chair scrapes loudly on the floor. Marnie looks up, ready to say something. Julie is blinking quickly, her mouth flapping open like a dying goldfish.

"We're going to be late," I say instead. "Thanks for letting me stay last night, Julie."

Julie nods stiffly. "It's my pleasure."

I pick up my bag, hugging it against my body, and leave the room. My coat is in the hall. I pull it down from the hook with clumsy fingers. The whole flat seems suddenly small and I need fresh air – big, fat gulps of it.

I move back down the hall to see if Marnie is ready – and as I do I hear hushed voices in the kitchen.

". . . I was only saying. . ." (Julie)

"Well, don't. She doesn't need it." (Marnie)

"Poor cow, I was only trying to. . ."

I walk back into the room, enjoying the look on

both of their faces as they attempt to act all innocent. Marnie's burning red cheeks tell me that she knows she's been caught out.

"Let's go," I say brightly. "We've got stuff to do."

We walk quickly across the street and take the shortcut through the park. It's not much of a play area really – two swings and a chipped climbing frame – but I guess it's something. The kids use the area to skid their bikes on, or to play footie on the worn-out field beside it.

When Lois and I were younger, we used to lie flat on our backs on the patchy grass, circling the mud with our fingers, looking up at the sky and trying to make pictures with the clouds. Every time, without fail, I could see a man with a long nose. Funny, if I look up now it's just balls of fluff, no shapes at all. I always preferred coming here, being out in the open space. Anyway, it's not like I could bring Lois back to mine. It's been a very long time since my place has been "welcoming".

Of course, Marnie wasn't with us then, just me and Lois. In those days it was just us two, almost daring ourselves to be up close to the Mac. It intrigued us, like some kind of foreign land. We longed to fit in with the kids there. But of course, Marnie would never have done anything naff like just staring up at the sky. She would've been bored in seconds. Marnie was probably born cool.

"Why the hurry?" Marnie is trailing a bit, fiddling to do her coat up. "Are we meeting Lois at school?"

"Yeah, I guess so."

"So why were you in such a rush to get out?"

"I didn't like all those questions. I felt like I was back home."

Marnie snorts. "You should've just told her straight. Mum wouldn't have minded. She's a nosy cow sometimes."

"Yeah, well. It's done now."

There is another reason for me making us leave, and as we head through the gate and across the dried-up field, I can see that my efforts aren't wasted. Lyn is standing with a bunch of his mates at the back of the shops. I know that he meets them there, usually to exchange fags that they can sell to the Year Eights later.

Marnie suddenly wakes up. "Oh, of course."

Me and Lyn have been going out for a few months now. It's been going really well, but I still get the feeling that Lyn doesn't want things to get too full on. He doesn't like clingy girls. He's one of those laid-back types, where you never quite know what he's thinking. I just constantly hope it's about me.

"I didn't know he'd be here," I say casually, smiling inside.

"Yeah, right."

Marnie nudges me, grinning. She's just spotted Ben sitting on the wall. She really thinks she stands a chance with him, even though he's currently been on and off with some posh kid from another school. I really don't see what the attraction is. Ben has that shaggy kind of hair that always looks a mess. And he's much shorter than her (and she's short!). She's obviously got bad taste. The other boys – Joel, Dean, Sean and Callum – are all in Year Eleven too. I don't really know them; they all tend to blend into the same person – loud, sarcastic and flirtatious. Only Lyn is a bit different. He has that kind of vibe that means he doesn't need to follow others.

Lyn seems to sense us as we draw close and turns slowly. He wears the school uniform like a model student, yet it always looks so sexy and cool on him. His black hair is cropped short against his dark skin, and his eyes are the warmest brown I've ever seen, like chocolate cake. So gorgeous. Sometimes he actually takes my breath away.

"Kez," he says, "nice surprise."

"I stayed at Marnie's last night."

Lyn nods. He sees that as a pretty normal thing. One of the few things he knows about me is that I sometimes need to escape. I hang out with Lyn here, at the park, by the flats, quieter moments by the lake. I could never take him back to mine.

He reaches out and touches my cheek, which is a rare public sign of affection. I can feel my whole body tingle with excitement. I bring my hand up to touch his, longing to hold it there. He rests his arm casually over my shoulder; I can feel the warmth move through me. One of his mates, Joel – I think – sniggers, but I ignore him. Idiot.

"I was talking to the boys about my party on Saturday. You girls coming?" Lyn says.

I didn't know anything about a party. I try not to look too blank or too keen. "Might do, not sure."

Marnie steps up beside me. "Sounds cool. Who's going?"

"Pretty much everyone. Dad's away for the night, so the place is ours."

It would've been nice if he'd asked me privately, away from everyone else. Is it too much to want to be treated differently by him? Like someone special? I think of our private times when it's just us; huddled under the slide, kissing, walks along the Estate with our hands locked together. Why does he still not treat us like a couple all the time?

"We'll go, won't we, Kez?" says Marnie, nudging me.

"Yeah, of course," I say, trying to look casual. "C'mon, Marnie, let's go. We'll be late for Lois."

I shrug off Lyn's arm and as he turns to face me, I snatch his cigarette. I don't even like them much but I quickly stick it in my mouth, knowing his lips have just been pressed around it.

He grins back at me and I think I die a little.

Lois meets us by the school gate. As soon as we walk up the road, it's clear she's annoyed about something. Lois has never been very good at hiding her feelings. I've known her for years now. When she's wound up, her face becomes pinched; it makes her look hard, scary even. The thing is, she's really pretty – like, stop-the-traffic pretty and she knows it. The confidence just spills out of her. I can imagine her being a model or an actress, splashed all over a glossy magazine. If she wasn't my friend I'd probably hate her.

"Lo! What's up?" Marnie is in her face straight away.

Lois just stares. She has her phone out and is texting

someone. I'm not sure who. Hannah, maybe. Those two have been hanging out together more lately.

"You OK?" I ask her. My tiredness has turned into a full-blown headache now and I want to get inside and take something for it. A jug full of pills.

Lois raises her eyes. "Yeah, sure. I'm OK." She sighs, and hitches her bag up on her shoulder. "I just thought – well, that we were meeting at yours last night?" She is looking at me and immediately I feel a stab of guilt. Yeah, she was meant to come to mine. Watch a DVD – chill out. I totally forgot to cancel it.

"I'm sorry. Did you show up?"

My heart is beating fast now. Please tell me she didn't.

"I knocked but no one answered." She is seriously fed up now, glaring at me. "But you were on Facebook earlier and you said nothing about calling it off. Then Hannah tells me you were at Marnie's."

How would Hannah know?

Marnie looks at me, obviously seeing my confused expression. "Her mum drinks at the pub. You know what my mum's like for gossip."

I feel so angry I want to scream, yet I can't let myself because I'm getting death stares from Lois – who really is the last person I want to annoy.

"I'm sorry. It was a last-minute change of plan. I didn't think." I say.

Lois looks so sad. She shakes her head. "You should've just said. You could've come to mine. I'm on the next road, after all."

I can't answer that, because no answer would sound right. How can I tell her that I could never feel comfortable in her house? It's difficult to explain why, because her family are so lovely, but I just struggle to relax. Her house mirrors mine in the inside; same layout, similar smells. In some respects her life even seems the same as mine, but it's not. It never will be.

"It was my idea. I'm sorry, Lois, I should've included you," says Marnie quickly. She raises an eyebrow at me, a kind of "what's the big deal?" look.

Lois shrugs. "Well, it's done now. I'm just kind of . . . I feel a bit, well. . ."

She seems to be struggling for the words but I know what she wants to say. Squeezed out. Unwanted. Left behind. None of these things are good. For a second, I squeeze my eyes shut to try and relieve the pressure that's building. I hate seeing her upset. I hate myself for screwing things up, but I just couldn't face going home. I didn't want to be anywhere near there.

I open my mouth to say I'm sorry again, that I

can make it up to her, but I'm stopped by Marnie jumping in front of me.

"Oh my God, get a look of that!"

I turn to see what she is pointing at and it takes a few moments for my mind to register the sight. Jess Pearson is running – if you could call it running – up the road towards us. She looks demented. Her arms are flapping around in the air, her thick legs seem to bending the wrong way – struggling under her weight – and her face is just a red, sweaty lump. Even her hair, which is usually scraped back, has forced its way out of its tight ponytail and is swinging round her face in wet, mousey strands. She looks hilarious.

We usually call her the stig, because in all honesty she is the most trampiest girl in school. If there was a competition for that category she would win first prize, no problem. Her clothes are old and ratty, her hair is greasy, it's really that bad. But today she looks even more gross than usual, and that's saying something. I really don't know why some people are nice to her. She is beyond help.

She approaches us, panting, coughing and choking. I step back, actually worried that's she's going to gob on my shoe. Or worse.

"Nice look," I say. I can't help myself. I'd die if I looked like that.

She glares at us and then passes me quickly. I know she hates us, it's written all over her face. But it doesn't bother me; she should take better care of herself. Doesn't she have mirrors in her house, or does she just not give a toss?

"Errgh, did the stig just touch you?" Marnie says in disgust.

I spin round quickly to face Jess. Did she just brush past me? Because if she did, that is rank – she is dripping with sweat and I don't want it on me. I stare at this breathless lump of a person, who is too frightened even to answer Marnie back. It's so pathetic. If she hates her so much, why doesn't she say something back? I can feel the pressure building again, but this time it's giving me a different kind of feeling. The burning, hot sensation in my head is now buzzing through the rest of my body.

So pathetic. How can you be so pathetic?

"Haven't you got something to say to me?" I ask. The words come out calm, despite my thoughts. I want her to bite back at me. I want to see some fire in that floppy belly of hers.

But she just looks at me, her mouth hanging open slightly. So I continue, "You shoved past me. I think you should say something." I'm pushing her. I know

I'm pushing her. I can see the tears pooling in her eyes making them look even more glassy than ever.

She says that she didn't touch me. She protests, weakly. She looks like she's going to sob hysterically. I can feel the rage burning even more. Why can't she stick up for herself? Why is she such a victim?

"On your knees and say it," says Marnie.

For a split second I'm shocked. Surely that's going too far. I see Lois's face and I don't think she's impressed. She turns around and starts playing on her phone again. But I know Marnie expects me to support her. She is staring at me now, makes a slight nod in my direction; it's my turn.

"Yeah, go on," I say, sucking hard on my cigarette and hating the taste. "In the dirt where you belong." But as I say it I'm thinking – nobody would do that, would they? No one would get on their knees? Not if you had any dignity anyway.

Which just proves that Jess Pearson has none, not one tiny bit, because she willingly gets down on the floor and begs for our forgiveness. She looks at the ground the entire time. It just proves to me she is a sad little freak.

So because of that we leave her where she belongs.

And I don't feel guilty.

I don't.

Kez Walker: Just got to keep smiling. Lots to look forward to ;o)

2 hours ago.

Like   Comment   Share

Marnie: Feelin better then?

Kez: Yeah. Guess so

Lyn: Ive ways of makin u smile. . .

Marnie: Lucky you

Kez: Things could be worse

Marnie: Yeah you could be Jessica Pearson!

Kez: OMG! Kill me now.

Marnie: I'm loading up the gun. . .

Kez: Plz do! I swear that would be the worst thing eva

Marnie: I'd rather not

Lyn: Nah . . . Jess is all right.

Marnie: Ah, give over Lyn she is rough

Lyn: You girls are harsh

Marnie: Trust me. We're right

Tuesday

You poor little cow. She offends my eyes. Big mistake.
On your knees and say it. This is not over. Please, please, please.
face. RIP. Have you looked in the mirror lately? There's nothing to worry. Fat.
This is not over. We need to talk. LOL. Evil. Gross. LOL. Fat.
Does she wash? Evil. Does she wash? This is not over.
You needed to. Fat. Poor little cow.
be taught a. please, please.
lesson. It's fine. You're pathetic. Fat. please. Evil. Gross.
On your knees and. There's nothing to worry about police
say it. Gross and. Evil. Next time I'm calling the police
Fat. Fat. Fat. RIP. you fat little freak.
You needed to be taught a lesson. It'll just make things wo
Have you looked in the mirror lately? It's fine, honest. RIP.

Jess

Another day. . .

I am thinking again about the messages I read
last night. I can't help it. I almost feel detached, not
quite part of all of this. I don't know, maybe I'm just
becoming used to it. After all, people like me aren't
designed to be loved and respected by others. Do I
blame Kez for not wanting to be me? No, not at all.

I don't want to be me.

I go into the bathroom to have a quick bath. I
wish we had a shower, that way I wouldn't have to
look at my body so much. I run it so it's only half
full and pour in some of Hollie's bubbles, as they're
great at hiding the flab. I pull off my nightshirt, still
looking straight ahead – I try not to look down
unless I have to. And then slowly, carefully, I ease
myself into the warm water.

I really don't know why I'm so fat. I don't eat that

much, I really don't. Mum says it's just because I eat the wrong things and maybe she's right. I do try not to. I really do. But sometimes I wonder if it's even worth debating; I'm obviously just weak, unable to resist the bite of chocolate or the temptation of crisps. If I was a stronger, better person I could say no. Mum buys treats for me and Hollie and then gets mad at me for eating them all. But I can't help it. It makes me feel better.

If I was a better person I would be thinner. And then I would be popular.

The bubbles are floating about on the hill of my belly, sliding down the shiny slope. I arch up my back, exaggerating the size. It's so large and white – I almost feel lost in it. Silvery marks, like tiny slug trails scar my hips. I run my fingernail across them, tracing the lines, the signs that my body is struggling. If I carry on eating, would these scars split open? Would my fat spill out like a slug's innards?

I wonder if it's actually possible to be trapped inside this flesh. Could delicate white bones be hiding under all this matter?

Help me! This blubber is keeping me prisoner. I'm trying to escape. . .

I pick up the pink razor that lies on the side of the

bath. Carefully I skim it over the pale flesh of my belly. I'm sweaty and my head is pounding. I press harder and see a tiny bubble of red emerge under the blade.

I lift the razor, staring at it for a second. So sharp, so powerful. I can imagine drawing it across my skin, letting all the bad stuff out. Turning the water a deep, angry crimson.

I'm worthless. I deserve this. . .

I press it against myself again, holding my breath. Then I let go. The razor floats harmlessly among the bubbles, bouncing gently against my leg.

I can't do this. I won't hurt myself. I won't. . .

The tears come before I can stop them. I cry silently, my hand pressed up hard against my mouth. I don't want Hollie to hear me. I don't want Mum to worry.

Mum is skinny. Hollie is skinny. I'm the odd one out. The spare part.

The mistake.

I'm not late today, which is good. I walk through the main entrance with no problems and have time to go the library before registration. It's quiet there. I can chill out for a few minutes, read my book. Or some mornings I can meet up with Phillip.

Phillip is probably my best friend. I'm so glad he's in a lot of my classes. Most people don't get him; they avoid him or give him weird looks. The truth is even I wasn't sure about him at first. Who would be? He dresses in a full blazer when no one else does, he wears the nerdiest glasses I've ever seen and he carries a bright orange rucksack.

Phillip seems to like being a bit different and I think that's cool. I like the fact that his hair is neatly combed (and no one can touch it) and his uniform is perfect. I love it that he taught me how to play chess (even though I'm a hopeless). He's so clever and is more interesting to talk to than most of the people in my year.

As I walk into the library, Phillip is sitting on the main table making a list. He looks up and then quickly away again. He rarely smiles.

"Hi, Jessica."

I sit myself down next to him. "What's that?"

"It's my list of the all-time best Shakespeare quotes." He pushes it towards me to show me. Some he has highlighted in yellow. "These are personal favourites."

"Oh," I nod, "looks great."

Phillip goes a little red and shakes his head softly. "Well, it's something to do."

I can tell that he's still deeply absorbed in the task, so I leave him to get on while I flick through my English book, *Wuthering Heights*. I'm still a little behind on it and am trying to catch up where I can.

Phillip looks up. "Not finished that yet, then?"

"No. I was hoping to, but Hollie hates me putting my lamp on at night and I don't like reading in the living room."

He looks at me blankly. Some things he will just never get, like the fact that I hate being on my own in the evening and will take myself off to bed as soon as Hollie does. That way I don't feel half as lonely. Once Mum goes out, our flat turns into a wide expanding space full of strange sounds and looming shadows. I can't help reminding myself that I'm only a brick width away from the outside.

"You could read the York notes, but it's nothing compared to the actual novel," Phillip says.

"Either way, I have to read more of it before English otherwise I'm screwed."

Phillip glances up at me; I can see his eyes have softened. He knows a bit about what's going on at home. "It's last period isn't it? Meet me at lunch and we'll talk through it."

"Really?"

"Yes. Sure. No problem. Meet me down in the lunch hall; we can talk as we eat."

I nod, pushing the book back into my bag. A tiny sensation of panic is just starting to nibble at the lining of my stomach. My first concern is that I have to eat in front of someone. Usually at lunch I take myself off to a quiet place to have my food – after all, who wants to see a fat girl get fatter?

But my second worry is that the lunch hall will be packed. And she will be there. Kez.

I'm really not sure I can face her today.

All morning, I carry around that horrible nervy feeling inside. It could be worse; I could have every lesson with them. But they are both in my Science and PE classes, which is a problem. Science isn't so bad, I can usually sit at the front away from them and just ignore the giggles, but PE is a different kind of hell. I'm hoping Mum will write me a note to excuse me – yet again.

At break, I go to the library again. Phillip's not there, he usually goes to the IT suite. But I'm pleased to see Hannah by the door as I walk in. Hannah is usually nice to me, even though she is friendly with Lois. I think it's because we were friends at primary school and Hannah's not forgotten this. She lives a few streets away from me. Years ago we played hopscotch on the chalked pavement between our houses. It wasn't so long ago that I could tell her anything. But then we came here, and everything changed.

"I thought I'd find you here," she smiles. "Do you always come at break?"

"Yeah, mostly," I smile back. My body is awkward next to Hannah's perfect skinny one. I would absolutely die for her long blonde hair, which is dead straight, like a Disney Princess. I guess her face is what you'd call more average-looking. Her eyes are small and heavily made-up, her nose is wide and her skin is very pale and bumpy, where she has attempted to hide her spots under clumps of foundation. I think she's trying to fit in too.

"Have you been on Facebook?" she whispers, her face creasing up in concern.

I nod, dipping my head so that I don't have to see the pity in her eyes.

"I just wanted to say that I'm sorry they're being like this. It's not nice." She moves closer to me. "My mum says you can report it. It's bullying. Maybe you should?"

I really want to laugh in her face. Honestly, has she a clue what's it like? It's bad enough being an ugly, fat freak. An ugly, fat sneak would be even worse.

"I don't think Lois likes it," she says softly. "But don't tell her I told you that. I think she's scared of Kez finding out and starting on her."

I look up then. I can't help myself. Kez and Lois used to be stuck together like glue. Why would she be against it? "What's she said?" I ask.

"Not much. I think she thinks it's going a bit far. She told me last night that they should leave you alone."

"Do you think they will?" I ask.

"I don't know. Maybe. Honestly, I haven't a clue." Hannah is looking shifty now; her eyes are flicking over towards the door. "I should go really, I'm meeting Lois."

"Oh yeah, don't risk being caught talking to me!" I spit. The words come out a little too loud and a Year Seven boy by the main bookcase looks over at us, a puzzled expression on his face.

"I'm sorry, Jess. I don't mean it to sound like that. I'm trying to help. Really I am."

She flashes me a smile, before slipping back out the door. I think it's meant to be an "I'm on your side" smile, but I could also read it as "rather you than me".

I walk to the far corner, wanting to hide away. And then I remind myself that I can't push people like Hannah away.

I need all the friends I can get.

The bell rings at the end of French. I shove my books in my bag, fumbling. Usually I rush to get to the lunch hall so that I can grab my food and run. But today there's no point in doing that. Phillip is in PE so will be over much later. I can't bear the thought of being in the hall on my own for too long. There's Hannah of course, but I know she probably won't want to sit with me. My best bet is to find a place with some of the less popular Year Eights, who might tolerate my company.

As I walk past Ms Noble she smiles. It's one of those sympathetic smiles that adults always give victims. I've got used to it now. It's like the little pats on the arm and the murmurs of understanding that they give. When I first got teased about my weight at the end of Year Seven – at the time, mainly by the boys – I used to report it regularly. I truly believed that, eventually, they would get the message and stop. I would open my heart to the school nurse, Janice, who although very sweet and happy to listen, would always end the session by suggesting diet plans and healthy-eating programmes. Sweet Janice. What could she know about it anyway? She is as skinny as a twiglet.

I slip into the hall and join the queue at the back, standing behind some older boys. They are loud and intimidating and I immediately want to leave again. One steps back and elbows me in the side. It's an accident, but they laugh. I shrink back, my cheeks burning up. I turn my face away, not wanting them to see me. It's times like these when I wish I could just evaporate.

"All right, Ben, don't get too close – you're making her blush."

I look again and realize it's Lyn speaking. I didn't see him at first as he had his back to me. A small smile escapes me, I can't help myself. He's always had that effect, even when we were little.

"You all right? Did I say something funny?" He says this loudly and his friends laugh. My stomach plummets to the floor. This could be bad. Is he pretending he doesn't know me?

"No. . . It's nothing." I stammer.

He smiles and then suddenly swoops forwards so his face his right in front of mine. I can smell his smoky breath and want to back away, but don't. "Don't be daft, Jess. You've gone all red. Are you OK?"

Relief sweeps through me. It has been years since we last spoke properly. We've both taken such different paths and I tend to avoid him now, especially since he's hooked up with Kez. I usually walk past him with my head dipped, avoiding all eye contact. After all, why would he want to be seen with me?

"How's your family?" he says.

I shrug. "Not great. Mum's stressy these days. Dad left us."

Lyn nods softly. "Yeah, I did hear that. My dad told me. He was just saying the other day that he doesn't see him down the pub any more. Look, I'm really sorry."

"Don't be. It's not your fault."

Lyn nods. "Well, I guess these things happen. You still in the bigger house at the back of the Estate? Do you remember when we used to play in your garden? It seemed huge. I was always so jealous."

I dip my gaze again, as I can remember being

in the paddling pool with him semi-naked. God, imagine that now! I was what? Four? So long ago. I loved that house; it was still on the Mac, but much bigger with a proper garden and everything. In those days everyone seemed happier. I swear when I think back everything seemed sunnier somehow.

But then of course Dad left and the clouds came.

"We had to move out," I say instead. "I'm in a smaller flat now, in Bevan Court."

"They're OK. You're lucky. At least you're not still stuck in the terror towers like me."

He obviously hasn't been inside one of the two-bed ones. There's barely room to keep a cat, let alone swing one. Obviously I don't say this.

A small smile is settling on his lips. "Anyway, you're still one of us. A Mac girl." I swear I'm glowing. I nod, try and make it seem like no big deal.

His friend Ben leans in towards us. His face looks pinched and evil. I start to feel uncomfortable again. I knew this was too good to be true.

"Surprised you'd fit in a flat that small. Don't you knock everything flying?"

For a split second I want to run away, like I always do. Or duck my head. Or pretend to laugh it off, act like the "fat jokes" are fine by me. *Hey, mate, I've not heard that one before.* But then I see his face, his stupid rat-like face, and something in me just clicks.

"Ha. That, coming from Frodo! Shouldn't you be living in a hobbit-hole or something?"

I don't expect his friends to laugh too. But they do. Really loud. I feel my cheeks burning again.

"Frodo! That's great. He does look like that hairy sod. That's a classic."

Now Ben/Frodo is the one turning red. Not me. He is glaring at me. But I don't care.

"She always did have a good sense of humour!" Lyn says, tapping my shoulder. "Better than this lot anyway."

"Shame her body ain't so hot," mutters Ben/Frodo. The others start to snigger. I can feel my earlier confidence begin to melt away.

"Oi!" Lyn says, scowling at them. He turns back to me. "Don't listen to them. They talk rubbish. You're looking great."

I only wish he'd said that a bit louder so that his friends could hear. I only wish I could believe it. I see something in his eyes. Is it pity? Does he know what they all say about me? He must know what Kez thinks of me, surely? When we were friends, it was different. We were little. We argued over Disney movies and shared giant ice pops. Besides, we were both chubby then. . .

The line shuffles forwards and I keep my head turned away from the main hall, worrying that Kez may appear at any time and break the spell. I pray that Phillip comes soon and we can disappear together, talk about books in the safety of our nerdy hideaway corners.

It's Lyn's turn to move over to food counter. As he goes to walk over, he carefully leans backs and whispers to me, "Keep smiling, dimples. Seriously, we should hang out again. It's been way too long."

Despite myself, a piece of me dies of happiness.

Have you looked in the mirror lately? Does she wash? Gross. You better show your face. You fat little freak. Fat. Fat. Fat. You fat little freak. It'll just make things worse. Please, please, we need to talk. Evil. RIP. She dresses like such a freak. Please Fat. Fat. Fat. Gross. and say it. It's fine, honest. Yeah, whatever. It's fine, honest. You fat little freak. Cow. Big mistake. LOL. Gross. Have you looked in the mirror lately? She dresses like just make things worse. such a freak It's little cow. LOL. Big mistake. Evil. There's nothing to worry You fat little freak. It'll just make things worse. Have you fat You poor little please, please Nxt time i'm calling the police. You're pathetic. This is not over. There's nothing to worry about. On your knees and say it. Gross. You needed to be taught a lesson. You fat little freak. RIP.

Kez

I'm starving and the canteen is full to bursting already. Typical. I look bleakly over at the queue and see that Lyn is right at the front. My heart leaps, which annoys me. I'm no good at playing it cool.

But maybe he'll get me some lunch. Save me having to line up. I hate standing alone, it makes me feel exposed. I will him to turn round and notice me, but of course he doesn't. Sometimes I think I would need to be wearing a bikini and be draped head to toe in fairy lights for him to notice me.

I move towards him and then I see that he's talking to someone. For a moment my brain can't quite take in what I'm seeing. He's laughing with a girl. And she's laughing back. It's Jess. The stig.

He knows I can't stand her. Is he doing this to wind me up or something?

I rub my temples. I know I'm getting twitchy,

nervous even. This isn't right. I wish Marnie was with me, but she's at a drama meeting and won't be here for another twenty minutes or so. I can't walk over to him now. He might be cold with me in front of Jess. I can't face that.

I can't believe she's laughing like that. I've never seen her look so relaxed and happy. She looks so different. Cocky, even. Does she know Lyn's with me? Probably. This must be some kind of sick joke.

I hang back for a bit, getting my phone out and fiddling with it. I could sit with Lois, but she's still in a mood with me. Pippa is waving at me. She's good fun, but a bit of a gossip. I wave back, realizing I must look really odd and awkward. I want to walk over to them, but my eyes fall back on Lyn.

Lyn is now at the counter with Ben and some others. Jess is still in the queue. She has her back to me. I flash her a look of pure evil anyway. How did she manage to make him laugh like that? He's never laughed like that with me.

Finally, Lyn is walking over to a table, carrying a tray, still deep in conversation with Ben who scuttles beside him. I don't know what Marnie sees in him. I put my phone away and casually walk over to them. I want this to look accidental, like they've just crossed my path.

"Hello, you," I say as I approach. Lyn lifts his head and smiles at me, slightly cocky, but still sweet.

"Hi," he says. "Good day?"

"Not bad. Getting better."

I want to kick myself. That's so naff. If Marnie was here she would be ramming her fingers down her throat. Lyn just grins. I think sometimes he looks a bit arrogant, just by the way he stands and the way his lip curls slightly when he listens to me; but I love this about him. I like the fact that he's slightly remote, it makes me feel like he's worth fighting for. He's a prize that I really want to win. It's no wonder Jess was enjoying talking to him, he's so much better than the geeks she's used to being around.

"Aren't you eating?" he asks.

My eyes flick towards the queue again. It's still really long; I'll be waiting for ages, on my own like the biggest loser. Jess is at the front now, loading her plate with chips no doubt, she usually does. Being fat obviously doesn't bother her. Shameless.

"I'm not really hungry," I say, but I steal a chip from his plate anyway. Lyn raises an eyebrow.

"I'm goin' to sit with the lads," he says. I can see his mates looking over, suddenly interested in our conversation.

"Can I come sit with you?" I ask.

He looks at me for moment, like he pities me or something. "Where's Marnie? Don't you usually hang around with her?"

"She's got a drama meeting now."

"Well, surely you're better off sitting with your mates? You always get bored sitting with us."

It's like he's taking all of the air out of me. Surely he knows that I just want to be with him. I feel shapeless and unwanted. Why does he suddenly not want me around?

"OK," I say, trying to remain casual, "I'll catch up with you later."

"Sure. I'll call you or something. You can tell me what sexy outfit you're going to wear on Saturday."

He turns and walks towards his table. I don't want to keep standing there, but something is keeping me rooted to the floor.

A few seconds pass, slow heartbeats in my head, and I make myself move away. As I do, I see Jess is sitting on her own at the back of the room. She is watching me, small beady eyes. I wonder how much she hates me.

I glare back at her, before striding out.

*

"She's taking the mick," Marnie says.

We are walking around the quad. There is only ten minutes left until the end of lunch and Marnie is sharing her large bag of crisps with me. At least my stomach no longer feels so raw.

"Do you think she knows I'm with him?" I ask.

"It's hardly the best-kept secret. Your tongue practically falls out every time you see him."

I laugh. "That just means I fancy him. And I do, who wouldn't?"

Marnie shudders. "Err, no. Too moody for me. But I think our little friend might."

She gestures towards the benches in the far corner. Jess (Stig-face) and one of her little friends are huddled on there, looking at a book. So dull.

"Who's she with?" I ask.

"Phillip 'bender-boy' Thomas. Don't you recognize the skinny freak?"

I nod, of course. They make quite an odd couple sitting there. But I guess they say opposites attract.

"C'mon," says Marnie, walking over.

Jess looks up as soon as we approach. I notice how her face turns a ghostly white straight away. I'm surprised she doesn't start shaking there and then. Her bottom lip drops open slightly and I can

see her chin and cheeks start to wobble. *Jeez, girl —
you're such a state.* Phillip on the other hand is still
reading. I'm not sure if he just hasn't noticed us, or
can't be bothered to look up.

"Care to join us?" he asks in a bored tone, still
reading.

I sneer at him. *Stupid freak boy, who does he think
he is?*

"Not really," says Marnie lightly. "We just wanted
to have a little chat with Jess." She purrs the words,
each one dripping with intent.

"Perhaps she doesn't want to talk to you," he
turns the page, head still bent.

"She can speak for herself, can't she?" says Marnie
sweetly, staring straight at Jess. She is sitting looking
at the floor, biting her lip. I bet she's dripping with
sweat. Disgusting.

"She certainly didn't have a problem talking to
Lyn earlier," I say.

Jess lifts her head. She blinks hard a few times,
looking straight at me. "Lyn?" she says, as if testing
out the word. "Lyn. But I've known him since I was a
kid. We were just talking, that's all. It was nothing —
honestly."

"What?" I bark, already irritated.

"It's just ... I said I knew him. . ." she is stammering now. "I – our dads were best friends, that's all. Not any more though. We both live on the Mac and used to play together, years ago. But, of course he's your boyfriend, isn't he? I swear, we were just talking." She blinked again and swallowed. "Nothing else."

"Oh yes," I say, leaning forward. "He's with me. So keep your fat, sweaty hands off."

She is still staring at me. Her cheeks now turning the shade of salmon. She shakes her head. "I didn't. . ."

"I'm sorry," Phillip suddenly barks, slamming down his book. "What exactly are you hassling Jessica for? Talking to your boyfriend. Is that not allowed?"

I switch my attention. Phillip is sitting facing me now, his face totally expressionless. He is beyond geekness with his stupid flat hair, neatly pressed clothes and naff bag. "I don't like her flirting with my boyfriend, no," I tell him.

Jess dips her head again, still protesting. "I wasn't. It wasn't like that. Honestly. Ask him?"

"Don't worry, I will."

"He's probably still traumatized by it," Marnie sniggers.

"Are you telling me you're that insecure, you have to threaten someone for simply talking to your boyfriend?" Phillip asks. "Didn't you hear what she said? They were friends long before you two even got together."

"I'm not insecure," I say. "What a joke, coming from two weirdos like you."

"Weird I might be," Phillip says, standing up. "But at least I'm happy with who I am, unlike you. Come on, Jessica, let's walk to lesson."

As if on cue, the bell goes, echoing around us in its shrill, piercing manner. All around us, people are rushing to class. A teacher screams over at us to "get a move on". I wait as Jess scuttles after her lanky "freak-friend".

"You better watch yourself," I hiss after her, noting how her back and shoulders tense at my words.

Marnie grabs my arm and we start to walk towards the main block, late as usual. I listen as she drones on about drama and her part in the new *Oliver!* production.

I just wish I could shake Phillip's words from my head. What the hell does he know anyway?

Freak.

*

Home. Jeez, how I've *really* started to hate this place.

It looks all right outside. People think I'm lucky, living in a neat terraced house with plants around the front door. It's funny how the problems can be shut away. Hidden neatly from everyone's eyes. Sometimes I think that's so much worse. It's not like I want my life outed on some naff TV show, but it would be nice if we could drop the stupid pretence for once.

I push open the front door. It's not late, just gone eight. They can't be mad at me this time. I've done what they asked.

The music hits me as soon as I walk into the dimly lit hall. It's the same rubbish he always puts on when he's in one of his better moods; some indie crap from when he was my age. If I come in to this, things will probably be all right. I can feel a small weight drop off me.

There's no point avoiding it, so I step into the living room. Dad is spread out on the sofa, the CD remote control resting precariously on his large belly. A hairy arm hangs loosely down, skimming the carpet. He's singing along. Loud, tuneless words.

I step in. "Dad. Where's Mum?"

He doesn't turn, doesn't even bother to look at

me. There was a time, years ago, when he used to scoop me in his arms and ask me how my day was. I haven't forgotten. I wonder if he has. I guess we're both different people now.

"She's popped out, be back in a minute."

I stand there, feeling useless. The music is vibrating on the soles of my feet. I wonder if Mrs Fletcher next door will complain again. The last time she did that Dad was in a rage for hours and we never heard the end of it. I hope she's out. "Don't just stand there. Fetch me a tea," he says and then starts singing again.

I walk through into the kitchen and flick on the kettle. It's spotless in here, it always is. I daren't even leave a dirty teaspoon in the sink. I open our fridge. Mum has stuffed it full of healthy food – salad and stuff. She's on another one of her diets. On the bottom shelf are beer cans, on their sides like large, cold grenades. He doesn't drink them all the time. But when he does things are usually much worse.

I carefully make his tea. I use his favourite Chelsea mug. Stir the teabag forty times, no more, no less. I watch as the dark water swirls around the soggy lump of a bag. Two heaped spoons of sugar and just a hint of milk. He says he likes tea you "can stand a teaspoon up in". To me it just looks dark and angry, a lot like him. I wonder if it stains him inside. Once I made it too milky and he threw the cup against the wall. It took me ages to get the stain out of the carpet. That was a particularly bad day.

I think I might actually hate him.

I place the cup carefully on the table beside him, making sure I use the coaster. On Saturday, I spilt a tiny bit. I didn't hear the end of that for hours.

Clumsy, inconsiderate bitch. . .

He looks up at me and nods, slow and grudging. His lips are pulled into a sneer. He reminds me of a bear, but not a friendly one like Winnie the Pooh. Lois has a dad like a teddy bear, a friendly, cuddly one. My dad should be kept in a zoo. He closes his eyes and goes back to his music. He has no interest in me now.

I barely register the front door opening and Mum walking in. But then I see the Co-op bag clutched between her thin fingers and I know what she was sent out for. His cigarettes and yet more cans. We live our lives around him.

"This is pathetic," I hiss at her, barging my way past. I make her wobble off balance.

"Where are you going?" she says. She looks at me with those wide blue eyes that take over her tiny, bony face. I swear I'm losing a bit more of her every day. A puff of wind will blow her inside out like a useless umbrella. Even her hair is more candyfloss than curls.

"I'm going out," I say, grabbing my bag again. I need to get some air. I just know I can't be here.

"But you've only just got back?" Her voice is whiny, pleading. She needs me here, I know that, but I can't face it. She puts the bag down. I see the light reflecting off the cans inside and want to kick them across the room. Why does he need more? More beer spells trouble.

"What's the point of talking? He's bad enough at the moment —" I gesture towards the living room, " — and you're just encouraging him."

Her eyes drop. "He just said he wanted more for later. It's been a tough day."

"But he has enough in the fridge. Why does he need more?"

"You don't understand," she says lamely.

"No, I don't!" My eyes are drilling into hers. Why does she let this happen?

"What's going on?" Dad's voice booms over the music.

"Nothing, Stu!" Mum shouts back. She turns to

me. "Please, Keren. Please come inside. You can't keep walking away."

But I grab my jacket and leave, hearing Dad's shouts behind me as I slam the door.

Like I said, it's easy to shut the problems away.

"Hi, Lyn."

I can hear his soft breath on the other end of the phone. "Hi. Where are you?"

I don't think I can tell him that I'm in the Mac. He'll just think that's weird, like I'm stalking him or something. I'm not. My feet just took me here automatically. Now I'm staring up at the grainy, graffiti-stained buildings of the Macmillan Estate. I know he lives up in the flats on the main block. I even know he's on the seventeenth floor, he told me once when he was boasting about the view. But he's still not taken me there. I wonder if he ever will.

"Just getting some fresh air," I say.

I walked away from my tidy little house nestled in the roads where Lyn never goes. I went through my wrought-iron gate, past my dad's battered Audi and down the tree-lined streets, with the neatly cut verges. I walked without even thinking. Ten minutes later and I'm here. Mum calls it hell. I call it real.

"Really? It's freezing out. Rather you than me."

I wonder what he's doing. Probably playing Xbox or chatting online. *What else do you do when you're alone, Lyn? Why do I feel like I don't really know you at all?*

"I just wanted to hear your voice," I say softly, squinting up at the brightly lit windows of the tower. I can picture the families inside; sitting down to the TV, all snug and warm.

"I've got a good voice," he growls, and I laugh.

It is pretty cold now and my light jacket isn't much use. I jiggle around a little, watching as the street lights dance in front of my eyes, creating hazy waves in front of me. I like being out at this time, the border between light and dark. Everything seems softer somehow, all the edges blurry, like the hard lines have been smoothed out with a rubber.

"I saw you talking to Jess earlier." I didn't mean to. The words just tumble out.

"Jess? Yeah, she was behind me in the queue today. I've not spoken to her in ages."

"Say something funny, did she?"

There's a pause. "Look, Kez, I know you don't like her or whatever, but she's a nice girl, OK? Bit shy maybe. I really don't want to be dragged into one of your bitchy catfights, but I don't see why you've got it in for her."

I snort. "It's not a catfight. She's weird. Did you seriously look at her? I know you two used to play together or whatever, but honestly – would you go near her now?"

I can hear him tapping now, obviously on his stupid computer. "That's harsh. There's nothing wrong with her. You and Marnie are bang out of order. Just because she's not stick thin." He sighs. "Honestly, I hate girls sometimes."

"You just don't get it," I say. "She could make more effort."

"Well – whatever, get over it. I wasn't chatting her up or anything. She just said something funny. I'm allowed to talk to other girls, aren't I?"

Yeah, yeah . . . just not her! I can still hear him tapping. I think I'm losing his attention.

"So Saturday's all sorted?" I ask, biting back the shivers.

"Oh yeah. It's going to be amazing. You'll be amazing. You always look good, you know that."

The blood is pulsing in my ears. "Really, do I?"

"Yeah, course you do. I'll be proud to show you off."

Show me off? Did this actually mean he's feeling more serious about us? A thousand thoughts are fighting for attention in my brain, but I take a deep breath and lift my head towards the milky sky. Above me a few stars are twinkling. I know this could be a hugely significant moment.

Or it could mean absolutely nothing. . .

I remember watching Dad playing poker, one of the few things he still loves. He sits with his hand held close to his face, his expression as blank as the back of the cards.

Never give yourself away, Kez. Never show your weakness.

I can taste smoke on my breath. And grit.

"I have to go now," I say. "I just wanted to speak to you."

"Night, babe," he says back and I wait until I see the screen on the phone go dark. He's gone.

Yet I don't go straight away. I stand rooted to the spot, staring up at the dark towers.

Wishing I had a different hand to play.

Kez Walker: Got to stop letting the little things get to me. . .

    1 hour ago.

    Like   Comment   Share

    Marnie: Or the BIG things. Lol

    Kez: Yeah. ;o)

    Lois: ???

    Marnie: Stig upset Kez 2day

    Kez: Nothing really. Just winds me up

    Lyn: . . .Baby, don't stress. Ruins your pretty face.

    Kez: Aw

    Lyn: Told u theres nothin 2 worry bout. AND B NICE!

    Kez: I know. But she winds me up. And did you see her hair today? Does she ever brush it?

    Marnie: Likes the wild look

    Lois: Oh I see this again. . .

    Marnie: Sorry Lois r we borin u?

    Kez: least we say what we think

    Lois: Yeah whatever

Wednesday

You poor little cow. She offends my eyes. Big mistake.
On your knees and say it. This is not over. Please, please, please.
face. RIP. Have you looked in the mirror lately? There's nothing to worry
This is not over. We need to talk. Evil. Gross. LOL.
Does she wash? Evil. Does she Evil. This is not over.
We need to talk. LOL over. wash? Fat. Poor little cow
You needed to Lol. please, please
be taught a lesson. please. Evil. Gross.
lesson. It's fine, honest. You're pathetic. Fat. worry about the police
On your knees and say it. There's nothing calling the police
say it. Gross. Fat. Fat. RIP. Evil. Nxt time I'm fat little freak.
We need to talk. Gross. LOL. You better show your You needed to be taught a lesson. It'll just make things worse.
3 We need to talk. Gross. LOL. Fat. Fat. Fat. Big mistake. Gross. Fat. Fat. Fat.
You needed to be taught a lesson. It'll just make things worse.
Have you looked in the mirror lately? It's fine, honest. RIP.

Jess

"Why can't I have Rice Krispies again?"

Hollie is really whining now. She's already driving me mad and it's only breakfast time. The empty packet is sitting between us like a tatty barricade. She keeps banging the side of it in protest, like doing that would magic up more cereal.

"Toast," I say. "There's enough bread for toast."

For you anyway.

I shove two dry slices into the toaster. It stinks of burnt crumbs. I swear one day this knackered thing will electrocute me. It must be about a hundred years old and has rust creeping up the corner like a nasty stain. I find myself running my finger over the roughness. I like the feel. I'm not really concentrating anyway. I have half an eye on Mum's computer, which is blinking at me from across the room. I knew it was a stupid idea to check the internet last night. Why do I do it to myself?

"I don't want toast. I don't like toast." Hollie's pouting now. How did she get such beautiful full lips? It's not fair.

"Whatever," I mutter, watching the red wires heat the bread. My own stomach is growling and the smell of cooking bread is making it worse. I rifle through the cupboard above me and find some peanut butter. That'll do. I spread it on nice and thick. All the time Hollie is fake crying and still poking the cardboard box in frustration.

She gets the proper breakfast, while I get spoonfuls of peanut butter and a couple of dry digestives. I have a Mars bar in my bag though. I can eat that on the way to school.

Why did I log on? It's like I had to torture myself reading Kez's messages. And then there was Lyn's reply... He obviously really, really likes her. Maybe they laugh about me behind my back? Yeah, I can see it now...

I hear the door slam and Mum's footsteps down the hall. Faster this morning.

Mum walks in and stands in the doorway for a few seconds just watching us. Her skin still has a grey tinge to it, but at least she's not frowning. A smear of pink lipstick stains her lips.

"I'm so sorry," she says, seeing me sucking on the spoon. "I've been paid now. I'll get some bits in."

"Is that OK?" I say. "It's just we're out of nearly everything."

"I want Rice Krispies," says Hollie, but at least she's taken a few bites of her toast. She's not stupid.

Mum stares at me, her eyes fixed and cool. "I said I will. So I will. Tell you what; I'll even get us fish and chips tonight as a treat. What d'ya say?"

My stomach growls again. My brain on the other hand is considering the amount of fat in chips. It'll just flop straight to my stomach. But I have to eat something, don't I? And chips taste so good.

Hollie is already cheering and high-fiving Mum. What else can I do but nod as well?

I'm doomed to stay like this for ever.

"C'mon then, you better get a move on," Mum says, looking at me.

I nod, *yeah OK*. But first I need to log out of her computer. Knowing Mum she'll be on it herself once I'm out of here – and I don't want her to see what they've been writing. Glancing at the screen, I see the red notification telling me I've been tagged again. My skin goes cold. Is it Kez?

I click the link quickly, like it might actually jump up and bite me.

A picture flicks up; it takes me a moment or two to take it in. Slightly blurry images of two little children playing, blowing bubbles in the sun. One of them is me, chubby arms and legs shoved in shorts that are far too small and a boyish blue T-shirt. My hair is cropped and sweaty. I look just like a boy. Hideous.

The other child is Lyn, also in shorts but much cuter of course. He is tall, with caramel-coloured skin, smiling directly at the camera. I remember his dad taking the picture. I remember us both laughing as the bubbles popped in our eyes and mouths. It had been a good day.

I look up and see that Lyn posted this only minutes ago. Above it is the message – "old skool memories".

I stare again at the picture; at the fat, red-faced girl trying hard to blow the biggest bubble, looking like her cheeks might burst with the effort. She was trying so hard to impress her bestest friend in the world.

Why would he post this?

What does he really think of me?

I came into science early and chose a seat at the front as always. Kez and Marnie never want to sit there. As the class starts to file in, I begin digging about in my bag, pulling out books, making myself look busy. I don't want to see them. My head is full of negative thoughts.

I remember when Hollie was little she used to love playing hide-and-seek. For her, it was enough just to shove her podgy hands in front of her face.

I can't see you, so you can't see me.

If only that were true.

I hear their voices of course. Who wouldn't? Kez is roaring with laughter, she has quite a loud voice anyway. I'm not even sure she realizes its strength. My back stiffens, but I try and concentrate hard on my homework. Checking it over, making sure it's OK. I expect them to pass by me, to sit at the back where they always do, away from the scrutiny of Mr Jones. It's not like they make any effort in lesson.

But instead Kez flops down on the seat next to me. She throws her bag down on the workbench. It's no accident that it lands flat on my book.

"Sorry, Jess," she says in a sweet voice. "Were you reading that?"

I pull my book back. It's no big deal really. "Yeah, I was just checking something."

Kez leans over me. I can smell her perfume, really

sweet and heady. "Oh, look at you – homework all done. Aren't you good?"

I shrug. "I guess."

"You're gonna let me copy, right?" She doesn't even wait for my answer, just sweeps up my book and turns to Marnie. "Look what Jess has given us, saves us a detention."

Good old Jess. Aren't I the nice one?

I watch as the two of them giggle, copying my answers. They aren't even attempting to make any changes. Mr Jones isn't a complete moron; he's bound to work it out. We'll probably all end up in trouble now and that's the last thing I need.

As soon as he walks in, Kez throws the book back at me. It lands awkwardly on my lap and in an attempt to grab it, I end up knocking it on the floor.

"Clumsy. . ." Kez hisses.

I resist the urge to glare back at her and instead attempt to pick the book up as quickly as possible. As I'm bending over, I feel a shove in my side. It doesn't take much to knock me off the stupid wobbly stool that I'm perched on.

I fall on the floor in a heap, on my side, my skirt riding up my legs. The laughter is so loud, it's like everyone in that room is joining in. I want to cover my ears to escape. It's so mortifying; I can't bring myself to move from the floor. It's as if I'm stuck there, as leering, mocking faces peer down at me.

And *hers* is the closest.

"Jess, what are you doing down there?" Kez asks, with fake concern.

"Like you care," I mutter back.

Mr Jones is at the front of the class now. I can see his shiny shoes. He must spend ages polishing them.

"What's all this noise?" he booms.

"Jess is on the floor, sir," says Marnie.

"What are you doing down there, Jessica? Get up at once. This is a science lab, not a playground."

I pull myself up, aware of the sniggers. I seem heavier somehow and it seems to take for ever to get back on to the stool. My hip aches where I fell.

"What were you doing down there anyway?"

"Like a little piggy, you like to roll around in the dirt," whispers Kez. Her eyes are bright and piercing. She is daring me to challenge her. I turn away.

"I fell, sir," I mumble.

"Well, be more careful," he mutters and is soon distracted by his handouts. I sit there glaring at the grumpy old git. Why doesn't he see what's really happening? Why does no one else see?

"I bet you liked it down there," Kez hisses at me. "Judging by the state of you, you're used to living in muck."

I have fire inside my stomach, travelling up my arms, down my legs – it's prickling through me like bolts of electricity. I bite my lip hard and taste the blood, warm and metallic. The sharp pain hits me, like a soft buzz of energy. I bite harder. What the hell does Kez know, in her perfect little house, with her perfect little life? Looking down at my shapeless, worn skirt and school jumper, with holes in the sleeve, I can see what she sees. Everything about me is a mess.

"A haircut would be a start," Marnie adds. "Seriously, have you looked in the mirror lately?"

I'm not looking directly at them, but I can feel both their smiles burning into me. They're waiting for me to cry. They are prodding and prodding, wanting a reaction. I'm like an elastic band being stretched out between their fingers.

"I guess that style might come back one day," adds Marnie. "Although it's doubtful."

I start writing now, copying the stuff off the board. Mr Jones is droning on, staring straight ahead at the class. His eyes are glassy and faraway.

WHY CAN'T HE SEE?

"Your poor little sister stands no chance, does she?" says Kez coolly.

The elastic band snaps. "What?" I say, turning to face her. The fire is now in my face. Burning and clawing at my cheeks. I'm giddy.

Kez is grinning, her beautiful face as cold as ice. "I said your poor little sister stands no chance, with you as a sister. No wonder your dad ran off."

I stand quickly, the rush in my head overpowering me. The chair scrapes the floor, making a sickening screeching sound. Mr Jones pauses, mid-sentence. Finally, he notices.

"Jessica, what are you doing?"

I stare directly at Kez. The tears are now here. She is still calm. Watching my reaction, her expression is stone. Marnie just looks bored.

"Well?" Kez says sweetly.

I push past her and run out of the room.

I slip into the medical room quietly. Luckily today it is fairly empty. One Year Seven boy with a nosebleed sits in the corner, a tissue pressed up to his face. He is looking up at me like I'm some kind of freak. At least I don't have paper hanging out of my nostril.

Janice is sitting behind her desk. She smiles at me.

"Hello, Jess, not seen you for a while."

"I have a headache, a really bad one."

Janice gestures towards the chair. "Sit down; I'll get you some water. Do you want me to call home?"

I think of Mum, trying to sleep. She hates being disturbed, but today I'm past caring. "Yes, I don't feel good."

Janice taps away at the computer, bringing up my record. Her faces gives nothing away, but I bet she thinks I'm putting it on. At least this time she would be right.

"Have you taken anything for it?" she asks, still not looking at me.

I shake my head. She gets up and starts rifling through the First Aid cupboard. She pulls out a box and removes two small tablets which she places in my hand. I watch in silence as she pours me some cold water from the tap. We've been through this routine so many times now.

"Has something happened?" she asks as she passes me the plastic cup. I coil my hand around it; the tablets are still pressed in my other palm digging into the skin.

"No," I say flatly. "I just want to go home."

"You know you could tell me – if you were worried about anything?" Her face is adopting that stupid caring expression again, but it doesn't fool me. I've sat in this room so many times before. She only sees what she wants to see. The anger I feel inside is surprising me. Surely I should be used to all this by now?

"I have nothing to say. I just want to go home early. I feel crap." My words are short and crisp. I can see the boy with the nosebleed is still watching me intently. I want to push him away too.

In fact I want to push the whole world away.

Janice gives a small sigh and walks back to her desk. "I was young once, remember. I know what it can be like."

"Were you fat too?" I say.

"No, but there's always something, isn't there? People always find a weakness."

I stare up at her and wonder what her weakness could be. She certainly doesn't look like a victim. Is her nose slightly too long? Are her fingers a little too stubby? Or was she one of them? A Kez?

"Can you call my mum, please?" I say.

I watch as she taps out the number, see the

expression slightly redden when she gets hold of Mum – she won't be happy, especially if she was woken up. I can imagine her moaning on the other end.

"What do you mean she's not well? Can't she just stay there?"

Janice replaces the handset. "She was OK. But she did ask if you were still able to collect Hollie later?"

I pick up my bag, nodding. "It's fine."

"Make sure you go straight home," she tells me. "Mum said she'll be in bed, but you can let yourself in."

"I will."

"And, remember, I'm always here if you need me. You might be surprised to find talking actually helps."

I don't answer. I just flash her a "whatever" look. The other girls do it all the time, so why shouldn't I?

As I leave I see the Year Seven boy is still staring at me. I stick my finger up at him and don't even bother to shut the door.

The corridors are mainly long and silent. It's weird when everyone's in lesson, the place seems different somehow. Calmer, I guess. The only things that remind you of the students are the occasional pieces of litter on the floor and the bright artwork on the walls.

As I turn the corner, I nearly run into two boys coming down from the Music Department stairs. My stomach drops when I realize one of them is Lyn.

"Hey," he smiles at me.

I flash a quick, not-too-bothered smile back and try and walk past. I don't want him to think I'm upset. I don't want anything getting back to Kez.

"Who's that?" I hear his mate say behind me.

"Oh, just someone I used to know," he says.

I keep walking, my face burning.

Someone I used to know. . .

In this area most of the artwork is by my year. My eyes glance at the names. A floral picture by Hannah. Phillip has done some computer-aided work with plenty of squares and bright colours. In the centre is a beautiful self-portrait by Ishrat, probably the best artist in the school. And then there's Kez's.

I stop now to look at it, because I'm quite surprised. I've not really noticed it before, but I'm amazed she could be capable of anything like this. It's pretty simple, quite bleak really – a bridge overlooking a railway line. Brambles and nettles tumble over the steps like long, twisty arms and the metalwork is rusty and brown, rotting into the ground.

I recognize it. It's the railway bridge on the other side of town. It's not been used for years since the small station was taken out of use. Kids sometimes play round there, but it's pretty dangerous, they reckon the bridge is close to collapse and is just waiting to be smashed down.

I wonder what made Kez paint it. It's hardly the most inspiring of places.

And then I see something else. A little girl's face, peering through the bars, down to the track. I push my face right up close to the painting.

I swear she's crying.

I don't go straight home. What would be the point? Walking into a small, cluttered flat where I'd have to stay as quiet as a mouse? Mum wouldn't want me there. I don't want to be there.

Instead I walk. The afternoon air is fresh and clear and I find myself moving at pace. I'm not thinking about where I'm going. I just let my feet lead me. I find myself coasting past the Mac, barely taking it in.

This is the estate where I grew up, but I feel nothing for it. The damaged, graffitied walls are like the burly arms holding the place together. I remember kicking footballs up against them, drawing pictures in chalk on the battered bricks. Once, I was proud to be part of it. As kids we would meet on the main field and spend hours playing "It" or Red Rover, while our parents watched from the grey-bricked houses and flats.

Then it didn't matter what size you were. You were part of the Mac and that counted for something. Scrap that, it counted for everything.

But then you get a bit older and none of that is relevant now. Half of us are desperate to escape these crappy walls and do something better.

There's no place for people like me.

I turn a sharp left by the park and keeping walking. I pass the pub (where Marnie's mum works), the community centre and the church. The church actually freaks me out a bit with its huge looming cross and windows, like all-knowing eyes. There is a poster pinned to the noticeboard by the gate. The letters are in red.

The one who conceals hatred has lying lips, and whoever utters slander is a fool

I picture a tightly pressed mouth trying hard to keep back the words they long to say. Could that be me? Another image of Kez comes to mind, spitting venom like a snake. Who's worse? I wish I could tear down the poster with its useless words.

I keep moving. The Mac is behind me now; the towering flats – the looming twins A and B – are in my shadow. I've reached the nice part of town, where the cars are half decent and the front gardens are neatly kept. Some houses even have names – like "The Willows" or "The Croft". What would they call our place if they saw it? "The Fleapit"?

Kez lives here somewhere. She likes to act like she's all hard, part of the Estate – but she's not. She's a nice little middle-class girl, living a pretty decent life. If only I knew her address. I'd hammer on her door and tell her nice little mummy just what a cow she really is.

Except I wouldn't, would I? Because I'm a coward.

I walk quicker, my chest is hurting, I even have a stitch. My feet slap on the pavement making hard, sharp sounds.

I walk until I reach number 32, "Beaches Rise", and then I stop.

Everything is the same as the last time I came past. The little hanging baskets, the Mini parked in the drive. I stand at the gate daring them to move, willing them to come out and see me. And then it happens, the front door swings open and out she steps. My dad's girlfriend. And then seconds later he walks out behind.

And he's holding a baby carrier.

Have you looked in the mirror lately? Does she wash? Gross.
You better show your face. You fat little freak. Fat. Fat. Fat.
You fat little freak. It'll just make things worse. Please, please,
we need to talk. Evil. RIP. She dresses like such a freak. Please,
Fat. Fat. Fat. Gross. and say it. It's fine, honest. Yeah, whatever.
It's fine, honest. You fat little freak. Evil. You fat little freak. Lol.
Big mistake. Lol. Gross. RIP. the mirror lately? a
she dresses like things worse
such a freak little cow. Lol.
Big mistake. Evil. There's nothing to worry it. You fat little freak.
It'll just make things worse. Have you looked you poor you please, please
Nxt time i'm calling the police. You're pathetic. This is not over. please. Gross.
There's nothing to worry about. On your knees and say it. Gross.
You needed to be taught a lesson. You fat little freak. RIP.

Kez

"GET OUT OF BED!"

He looms in the doorway, glaring down at me
like the Grim Reaper. I pull at the covers feeling
both hot and cold at the same time. My mobile is
blinking beside the bed. I glance over at it. It's not
late. Why is he freaking out?

"Did you hear what I said? Get up – now. I'm
sick of seeing you lazing about."

"I'm not lazing about. It's seven. I've just woken
up."

"What time did you get in last night?" His eyes
are like lasers burning through me. He's gripping
the door frame so tight the tips of his fingers are
turning white. This is not good. Not good at all.

"I went for a walk. Then I went to Marnie's." My
mouth is dry and the words sound thick and slurred.

"So what time were you back?"

"You were asleep. Half-ten, I think. I didn't want to wake you, did I?" I glare at him. I can't help myself.

"Your mum was worried sick."

"She didn't say nothing," I say, irritated now. Mum was there when I walked in, her nose stuck in her stupid book. She'd barely looked up.

"All evening she kept checking her phone. You use this place like a bloody hotel."

I pull myself up. My school clothes are thrown on the chair on the other side of the room. I grab them and move towards the door. "Excuse me," I say, barging him a bit.

"I'm talking to you. Don't think you can just walk off again."

"I need to get dressed. Or do you just want me to turn up to school like this?" I gesture at my faded T-shirt.

Dad's face is getting redder. I know I'm pushing it. "Where the hell is your respect, girl?" he hisses.

"This is my room." I finally manage to force myself past him. "You have no right coming in and having a go." I go into the bathroom and slam the door, quickly locking it behind me. Relief floods my veins. I'm surprised at how sweaty and breathless I am.

I can hear him thumping downstairs. His voice is like it's on loudspeaker. I sit on the toilet, listening.

"She's needs to learn some respect! I've had it up to here with her attitude!"

I can't hear my mum's muffled reply. I imagine she's trying to calm him down.

"I don't care what you say. You let her get away with bloody murder. You're spineless. Useless!"

There is a crashing sound, like breaking glass. I draw breath. I should be used to this but I'm not. My mum is screaming now.

"What did you do that for?"

"I can do what I like! It's my house!"

I move over to the shower and turn it on. The blast of water is fierce and loud. I strip off clumsily and step inside the protective glass. In here I can pretend they aren't killing each other. In here I make out that everything is OK. I turn my face into the jet of water and let the fine stream hit my skin. It stings, but in a good way. The tears are easing their way out of my closed lids. I don't bother to fight them. It's better that I cry here than later, in front of anyone else.

I dry and dress myself in the safety of the locked room, humming quietly under my breath. I take time at the mirror, carefully applying concealer to mask the dark circles, loading up the mascara, opening up my eyes. I continue singing so that I can't hear them screaming. I only wish I'd brought my iPod in with me. The lipstick is my final touch, the dark rich colour that makes me look strong, in control. I pull my hair into a tight ponytail away from my face. And then, when it's finally quiet, I creep out of the room and down the stairs.

I don't check what room they're in. I'm sure I can hear Mum softly sobbing somewhere. No surprise there, then. Luckily my school stuff is all waiting by the door. I open the front door and go outside, pulling the door shut behind me.

I doubt they've even noticed I've gone.

I hate science – mainly because I'm thick and don't understand it. I don't even know why they stuffed me in this set. I must've fluked a test or something. I'm not designed to be clever; my brains are just not made that way. Give me a paintbrush any day.

I only have to look at the diagrams on the board and I zone out. Wake me up when it's all over, or even better kill me now. Anything but be subjected to this.

At least I have Marnie to sit with. She pretends she doesn't get it, but she's smarter than me. Marnie doesn't like people to know that, though, because it's not cool. Sitting with her means we can have a laugh and maybe get some of the work done – if we can be bothered.

As we walk in, she pulls my arm.

"Let's sit with little Miss Stig Pig."

I burst out laughing. I can't help myself. She's joking, isn't she? Why the hell would I want to make this lesson even duller? But of course she's not joking and she drags me over to where Jess is sitting. Everyone else in the room is either talking or playing with their phones, but not Jess. She has her head stuck in her book and is busy scribbling away.

I ask her what she's doing and her whole face pales. She shifts over a little in her seat, like I smell or something. She says she's doing homework, catching up. Her fingers drift over a worksheet stapled in her book.

Homework? Oh no, was there? I'm so far behind that Mr Jones has put a note in my book telling my parents what a screw-up I am. Remembering that makes my stomach sink. I've managed to keep it hidden – for now. The next thing will be a call home and that would send Dad deranged. I really don't need the grief.

I take Jess's book and tell her I need to copy some of the stuff. She nods meekly. She's hardly going to say no, is she? But sometimes I wish she would. Just so she wasn't always such a pushover. Then I might respect her more. Marnie copies some stuff down and she doesn't even need help. She's just too lazy to bother doing it herself.

Then Mr Jones walks in, his expression is dark and unreadable. I throw the book back at Jess; if I'm caught with that I really would be dead. Jess does this weird flappy motion with her hands and manages to knock the book on to her lap. More flapping sends the book to the floor. Honestly, she is such an idiot.

"Clumsy," I hiss at her. I'm tempted to say more, but bite my tongue.

Jess's face is wild with panic – she leans over to reach the book. She looks so stupid, half hanging off the stool that I can't help giving her a soft little nudge, it's just too tempting not to. She falls, almost in slow motion – flat on her side. It's lucky she's quite big, because that would've hurt. I feel a bit bad. She's so pathetic down there and weirdly, she's not moving much – it's like she's actually dying of shame. Part of me just wishes she would get the hell up instead of making herself look even more lame.

"What are you doing down there?" I ask, trying to keep it light. Making a joke of it. I assume she will jump up, smile and brush herself down.

"Like you care," she hisses back.

I stare back at her, all sweaty and useless on the floor, and I can feel the anger rising inside me. Why the hell is she taking it out on me? It's not my fault her stupid, doughy hands can't catch for crap.

Mr Jones notices that something is going on and snaps at Jess to get up. He assumes she is messing around. I don't think he likes teenagers much; he looks at all of us as if we're something that's just dropped out of a dog's backside. Jess stands up. Her uniform now has dust on it from the floor, but she looked a mess anyway. Her skirt is all out of shape and far too long and her jumper has holes in it. She looks like she's been styled by Oxfam, and even that's being kind.

"I bet you liked it down there," I say. "Judging by the state of you, you're used to living in muck."

Marnie giggles next to me. I'm pleased that she's looking impressed. I'm not usually much good with the quick lines like her.

Marnie starts tearing into Jess now that I've sparked her interest. She points out that Jess's hair looks awful (it does) and she looks a complete mess (she does). Jess stands there and takes it. Her eyes keep flicking over to Mr Jones. I think she's hoping he will say something. She's such a little grass, I'm surprised she doesn't stick her arm up and report us. Or burst into tears.

"Your poor little sister stands no chance does she?" I say. I know this will piss her off. She's crazy about her sister, everyone knows that.

Her face changes then – goes all weird and hard. "What?" she says. She's looking directly at me now, she never usually does that. Her eyes are all starey and glassy.

I sigh, acting like this is boring me now, but it's actually getting interesting. I want to see how far I can take this. "I said your poor little sister stands no chance, with you as a sister. No wonder your dad ran off."

She keeps looking at me for a few seconds more; I'm surprised how long she can hold my stare. I'm also surprised at how green her eyes are. I've not noticed that before. It's a shame she doesn't do anything with them. They're wasted on her.

And then she just leaves, gets her bags and

storms out of the room, leaving Mr Jones in more of a flap than ever. She even barges me slightly as she goes – cow. I imagine she's running to the toilets or medical room for a good cry. Just as long as she doesn't report us, I don't care where she is. I prefer not having to see her soppy face.

"Was it something we said?" whispers Marnie with a grin.

"She's just weak as. . ." I hiss back.

I turn and notice she's left her exercise book behind. Without thinking I pull it towards me. On the front she's drawn her name in big bubble writing – like a kid would. Underneath she's drawn a neat little flower, a rose bud I think. It's quite clever.

"Urgh," hisses Marnie, peering over my arm, "she's so naff."

"I know."

I get my black pen and draw around her rose. It doesn't take long for me to turn her stupid little picture into a neat-looking gravestone. Complete with the words – *JESS R.I.P.*

She should get the message now.

The house is quiet when I walk in. That's not right. Dad's always home now. Where else would he be?

I throw my bags down by the door and can feel my whole body going tense. Maybe it's all right – he's probably just asleep. Or maybe he's actually got an interview. He's not had one of those for months now.

I slip past the living-room door. It's standing wide open. At first I think there's no one there and go to walk past. And then I see her, curled up in a ball on the sofa.

"Mum?"

I step inside slowly, keeping my voice lowered. Mum is facing the cushions. She sighs gently and turns. I see her face and it's like an invisible punch has struck me in the stomach.

"Not again," I say. I go over to her, not wanting to look at the swollen lip, the red nose, the eye that's closing against me. She looks such a mess, all bright colours that look so wrong on skin. I want to walk back out the door again. I wish I'd not had to see this.

"I'm OK," she says. Her voice sounds all muffled like her mouth is stuffed with cotton wool. "It looks worse than it is."

"Where is he?"

She tries to pull herself up, her good eye blinking

hard. "Out. I don't know where. He stormed out ages ago."

"Oh, Mum." I taste sick in my mouth. "Do you need me to get something?" I reach out towards her nose and retract as she flinches from me, "Surely we should get that checked? It might be broken."

"I'm fine! I told you. Stop fussing. A few days and this will all be forgotten. I've had worse."

Yeah, like the broken arm, do you remember that one? You told me that was your fault too — like everyone deserves having their bones snapped in two.

The buzzing in my head is driving me nuts. It's all I can do not to shake her and shout in her stupid cut-up face.

"You can't let him get away with this," I hiss instead.

"It's not his fault, Kez. You don't realize how stressed he is right now. We both need to give him a break."

"A break!" I spit. "You're joking, right? He's just smashed up your face."

Mum turns away from me. "I'm not talking about this any longer. All parents row. It's part of life. You'll understand that one day."

I step back, shaking. I have no words left. It's all

been said before. We both know she'll roll over and take it. We both know Dad'll do it again.

My heart lurches as I suddenly remember Dad standing at the foot of my bed this morning. That curled fist around my doorframe.

"This is because of the row with me, isn't it," I say. "This is my fault *again*."

Mum doesn't answer, but that's an answer enough.

I walk out of the room and shut the door quietly behind me. I just pretend I can't hear my mum crying. She's always crying these days.

I'm getting good at pretending that all this doesn't matter any more.

Kez Walker: Party soon. Can't wait. Just gotta decide what to wear. . .

23 minutes ago.

Like   Comment   Share

Marnie: Yea! Going to be so much fun. U look beautiful whatever you wear

Kez: Yeah – right ;o(

Lyn: Can't wait guys. Goin to keep the Mac awake!

Kez: Yeah!!

Marnie: Goin 2 b so cool. Cant wait

Lyn: Loadz goin now

Kez: You're brave

Lyn: Or mad. . .;o)

Kez: Can't wait Lyn Roberts. This will be the best night eva

Lyn: You betta believe it

Thursday

You poor little cow. She offends my eyes. Big mistake.
On your knees and say it. This is not over. Please, please, please.
face. RIP. looked in the mirror lately? There's nothing to worry
This is not over. We need to talk. LOL Evil. Gross. LOL.
Does she wash? Evil. Does she wash? This is not over.
We need to talk. Fat. Fat. Poor little cow
You needed to Please, please.
be taught a please. Evil. Gross.
lesson. It's fine, You're pathetic. Fat. worry about police
On your knees and honest. There's nothing to calling the police
say it. Gross and Fat. Next time you fat little freak.
You needed to be taught a lesson. It'll just make things wo
Have you looked in the mirror lately? It's fine, honest. RIP.

Jess

OK, so this wasn't where I was expecting to be at nine o'clock in the morning. I'm not even sure how I got here either. I dropped Hollie off as usual and then just kept walking. Thing is, I ended up walking past the school and into town and now for some reason I'm standing here at Smithy's Greasy Spoon. Maybe I'm having some kind of mental breakdown. Or something else is wrong with my brain, but I really don't remember walking here.

Dad used to bring me here when I was little. We used to sit by the window eating toasted teacakes and watching the world go by. He used to tell me you could spot "all sorts" in a café. He said one day he'd bring a notebook and write about all the characters and "make a mint" out of it. Yeah right, like he'd ever do that! Dad has never been one for sitting down and sticking to anything. Something else more exciting will always whisk him off and his ideas are quickly forgotten.

I think the last time I saw him properly was here. That was three years ago. He bought me tea and told me that I needed to be a big girl now that he was "moving on".

"Sally doesn't like children much, you see," he'd said, stirring his cup. "So it'll be harder for me to see you."

I'd wanted to tell him that I wasn't a child any more. I'd wanted to tell him that I still needed him around, probably more than Hollie who was happy, young and cute. I wanted to tell him that he was being totally unfair and that Sally was just being a nasty bitch. But I didn't, I just drank my tea and nodded stupidly.

It's clear now that Sally just doesn't like children that aren't her own.

I step inside Smithy's. It smells just the same as I remembered — rich with grease and coffee. Tinny music blasts from a small portable stereo on the back shelf. A woman with jet black hair pulled into a tight ponytail is busy mopping up tables. She moves quickly like a manic bumblebee, her face is gaunt and her cheekbones project out, dark shadows circle her eyes. She smiles at me as I walk in.

The nervousness is clawing at my belly. I shouldn't be here. I'm truanting. That could mean a serious fine for Mum. If she found out she would skin me alive, or worse. But I keep walking. I walk to the counter and stare up at the bright yellow sign on the wall behind, listing all my options. I have five pounds to put on my lunch card at school; I reach into my pocket and feel for it with my fingers.

The woman comes over. Her movements are awkward like her back is hurting. As if to confirm it, her hand goes round behind her and starts rubbing.

"Place will be the death of me," she moans. "What can I get you?"

"A tea?" I say, the words coming out all small, like a squeak. "And maybe some toast?"

"Sure? Jam or anything?"

"That'll be nice."

Mum didn't go shopping, so there was nothing to eat this morning. I had to give Hollie crisps and a slice of cheese. Mum swore she'll go today. If she doesn't . . . I don't know what I'll do. I was just lucky to find the five-pound note behind the breadbin.

I go and sit by the window. It's the same place I sat with Dad three years ago. The tables are a bit chipped and stained. I place my hand on the cool

111

plastic, remembering that his skin once touched here. I wish he'd scratched his name here; it would be lovely to see something that was actually his. Apart from my broken alarm clock, a few books and some tatty photos, I have nothing of Dad. Sometimes it's as if he didn't exist. Or is slowly being erased out of my life. I squeeze my eyes shut and I can still picture him sitting here, shaven head, bright blue eyes, huge arms. He has a tattoo on his hand, a small bird. When I was small I used to think it came alive at night and flew around the room.

He used to call me his little bird until I started growing big.

There's not many people to look at here, Dad would be disappointed. An old man sits in the corner reading a paper and occasionally picking his nose. A tall, young man dressed head to toe in denim sits by the counter fiddling with his phone. He keeps shouting things at the woman working here. I quickly learn her name is Lorraine. She glares back at him and snaps back short, bullet-like answers. I don't think she likes him much.

Lorraine brings me my tea and toast and even manages a bright smile, even though I can tell the denim man is really annoying her, especially when he shouts over that "she's a bloody useless cook".

"My boyfriend," she whispers, as she puts down my plate. "Take no notice."

I shrug. Poor her. I'm not sure I'd like to go out with someone like him.

"Shouldn't you be in school?" she asks softly.

I can feel my cheeks redden, but I take a bite of my toast. "I have an appointment this morning. They're letting me go in later. I just needed something to eat first."

"Oh, of course," she smiles. "To be honest, you looked too nice to be a skiver. They usually hang around later, smoking their fags outside the door."

I smile back.

Yes, I'm too nice.

"You're too nice to be with him," I say.

The word spill out before I can help myself. Her thin cheeks turn a bright shade of pink and I immediately feel the twist in my stomach, the expectation that something bad will happen. But instead, a small smile creeps upon her face. She immediately looks younger.

"You know what, you're dead right," she says.

I watch as she walks back over to the counter. As she passes the denim man, she flicks out her middle finger. Then she carries on walking through to the back. The man's mouth hangs open like a dog left out in sun.

I eat my toast slowly, enjoying every mouthful. As I do, I imagine Dad is still sat in front of me, stirring his tea and talking to me.

But this time he's not telling me he's leaving me. This time he's staying right here.

I'm not sure where else to go. At first I have every intention of going back to school. I even go right up to the gates. They would have been in third period by now, that would be Maths for me. I don't mind Maths. My foot lingered over the line dividing school and outside. Could I face it? Did I want to?

Then my eyes fell to the spot where they made me kneel. The dog poo was still there, rotting away on the edge of the grass. The ants were long gone. All the thoughts about what happened came rushing back to the surface and it was like I couldn't breathe. I ended up clawing at my neck, tugging at the tie. I had to pull it off in the end and stuff it back into my bag.

Then I just turned and walked away. I couldn't do it today. My whole body was fighting against it.

So where the hell could I go?

First I walk to the library. Luckily it's not far and I spend a few hours hiding in the reference section, writing out my History homework and trying to get to grips with *Wuthering Heights*. Then I realize I'm getting some funny looks from one of the workers and paranoia gnaws at me. I can't let them report me for truanting. I leave quickly, trying to look relaxed and natural.

This is normal. I'm just taking one day off – that's all. I'm not doing anything wrong.

I can't walk too far. I already have a blister coming up on the back of my foot; it's been making me walk funny. As I head up the hill, back towards the Mac, I'm aware that I'm dragging my leg a bit. I wonder if I look strange, out of place. Mind you, don't I always?

Coming back to the Mac might not be my brightest idea. There's a risk Mum might see me. Then again it's unlikely, she barely leaves the house. As I approach the towering blocks, which loom like greying Duplo blocks, I decide to head for the park. At least it will be quiet there.

The field itself is deserted apart from an old man walking his dog. He walks carefully, moving his hip like it's made of lead. The dog is a small yappy thing that looks at me with his bright, knowing eyes and delivers a short, strangled bark. The man tugs at his lead and mutters under his breath. He passes us without looking my way once. That's what it's like here. No one looks at anyone.

I sit down on the bench facing the play area. It's old and worn and the wood has all splintered away at the edges. People have carved their initials all over it, marking it for ever. Where I'm sat someone has written "DEADZHEAD", the letters are large and challenging. I run my fingers over the grooves. If I had a knife, or anything sharp, I would be tempted to add words of my own.

What would what I say anyway? Why is everything stuck inside me?

"Hello, dimples."

I look up, startled, wondering who the hell has come up behind me. I certainly don't expect to see Lyn smiling down at me; his hands slung in his jeans pockets. He looks almost shy, awkward maybe. His eyes seem tired, less sparkling. I wonder whether he's had much sleep.

"Hello," I say back. It's like sparks of electricity are dancing across my arms and back. I want to shiver but I hold back. "What are you doing here?"

"I was going to ask the same of you," he says, sitting himself down beside me. "I never took you for someone who'd skive off school."

"I don't. I just couldn't face it today." I don't look at him. I keep my eyes set on the deserted playground. It looks so weird when there's no one in it.

"I can't face it any day. Teachers are always giving me grief, reckon I'm going to fail my exams," he shrugs. "So what."

"Don't you care?" I ask.

"Nah. There's bigger things to worry about than some stupid qualifications. Where the hell will they get me anyway? I'd be lucky to scrape through."

"They could get you out of here," I say and then instantly regret it. The Mac is like the centre of the universe to most of the people here.

Lyn is really staring at me now, his eyes are so intense. "Is that what you want? To get out?"

"Yeah," I say. "Sorry, but I do."

"No need to apologize. Just hope you get what you want." He starts digging at the grass with the heel of his trainer. "Maybe you've got a chance. You're clever, aren't you?"

"I guess."

"Well, then. You shouldn't be missing school."

"Says you."

"Says me!" he laughs. "I do have good reason though, had something important to do."

I want to ask him what it was, but I sense a change in his mood. His shoulders are now slumped forwards and he's chewing hard on his lip. He carries on digging at the mud, harder now.

"This whole town is a hell-hole," he says finally.

"You're not wrong there," I reply, sitting back a bit.

He digs about in his pocket and pulls out some cigarettes. "Do you want one?"

"No, thanks."

"Oh, course not, you're a good girl." But he's smiling again at me while he lights up. "You don't mind if I do though?"

I shake my head.

"You get a lot of stick at school, don't you?" he says, still staring at me. He puffs hard on the cigarette; his face frowning like it tastes bad. I don't bother answering him. What's the point?

"I know they say stuff about you. I've seen it all on the internet," he says softly. "I don't get why they do it."

"Everyone's seen it. I'm getting used to it."

"You shouldn't have to put up with that. You don't deserve that." He's shaking his head. "I swear I don't understand people sometimes."

I frown at him. "You know your girlfriend is behind most of it."

Lyn shifts in his seat. "Yeah, well, that's part of the problem. I mean, we are going out. She's a nice-enough girl, but stuff like this does my head in. I'm not even sure. . ." He pauses, staring out into space like something has distracted him. "I can have a word with her if you like?"

I immediately picture Kez's reaction if Lyn were to challenge her. It was bad enough when she caught us talking the other day. I feel myself tense all over.

"No. Don't talk to her. It's fine. I can handle it."

"Well, as long as you're sure? Anytime. I can talk to her anytime."

Sure? Of course I'm not sure, but I don't even bother to answer that. My life now is just an endless game of avoiding trouble. Just as long as I can convince people stuff like this doesn't bother me, it might actually go away.

Yeah, just keep telling yourself that, Jess. Who is it you're really trying to kid here?

"I was with my dad today," Lyn says suddenly, his head still turned away from me. "He's not been well."

"Oh." I'm not really sure what to say, I know how close Lyn is to his dad. "Sorry to hear that – is he OK now?"

"Not really. He's in hospital. They're running tests, all kinds of things to find out what's going wrong. He keeps puking and stuff."

"That's not good."

Lyn takes his cigarette and grinds it hard into the ground. "It's life though, isn't it? You're born, you get ill, you. . ."

". . .recover," I finish for him. Before I know what I'm doing, I reach over and touch his hand. It's cool and rough. I expect him to pull away, but he doesn't. He's still staring straight ahead.

"So you have no idea what's wrong with him?" I ask.

"Nah. I don't think anyone does really. Like I said, they keep running these tests. Thing is, he smokes, drinks and he eats crap. It's no wonder his body's given up on him."

"Is your mum still not around?"

He shakes his head. "Nah. Auntie Pam is there

loads to make sure I'm OK – she's in a flat in Tower B now. But it's not the same; I just want Dad back home."

I remember Lyn's mum walked out on them when he was still a baby. His dad used to drop him round to ours when he was working. In those days my mum didn't have a job so she could look after both of us.

"We used to have fun, didn't we?" he says, now looking straight at me, like he can read my mind. His eyes are so deep and piercing; it makes my heart beat a little faster.

"You used to put worms in my hair," I say, poking him in the leg, "and you made me lick a snail once, do you remember? For a dare."

"Oh God! Yeah, I do. But you were evil. You used to break my cars on purpose! I swear those days were some of the best ever."

"But then you got all cool at school and that was it," I tease. "No more hanging around with the fat girl."

His eyes widen. "Don't think that, Jess. I was just older. I got into other things I guess. But I've never forgotten about you."

I can feel myself blush, so I quickly look away.

I feel stupid for feeling like this around Lyn. He was always like my big brother. Why did he have to grow up to be the popular, good-looking one?

"We all change," I say instead.

"Not really. Not inside. That's the thing, isn't it? You start to realize there's more to people than a ton of make-up and flashy designer clothes."

"I guess."

I'm staring at him, wondering if he's referring to Kez. But I don't dare ask him.

"Did you see the picture I put up? Of us?" he asks.

"Yeah," I shake my head, my cheeks burning. "I looked awful!"

"No, you didn't! You were dead cute. How could you look awful with those eyes of yours?"

I don't know what to say, I let a little grin escape, I can't help it. He holds my gaze for a minute and then pulls away, biting his lip.

"To be honest, I feel bad about having the party, but Dad says I should go ahead. He wants me to carry on as normal."

"So do it," I say.

He turns, his eyes are bright and I can see the hint of tears in the corners. "You're coming, aren't you?" he says. "I really want you there."

I stare back at him; I can actually hear my pulse racing in my ears. "You're joking? I won't be welcome."

He suddenly takes my hand and squeezes it tightly. "Yes, you will. Say you'll come."

I think of Kez. She'll hate me for this. This could finish me.

I look at his hand in mine.

"OK," I say.

He smiles back at me. "You shouldn't take any more stick. Stand up for yourself a bit. Don't be scared."

I nod, feeling a bit silly. But it's so easy for him to say.

"I need to go in a bit," I say instead. "I have to pick my sister up from school."

"Cool," he stands up and stretches. "You mind if I walk with you? I could use some company."

I'm tempted to look round me, check that Kez and Marnie aren't hiding in the bushes filming all of this. Is it just a trick? Another laugh at my expense? But something in Lyn's calm expression is telling me to trust him.

"Sure," I say.

He grins back at me. I'm sure I can see a flicker of

something in his eyes, almost as if they're softening in front of me.

The trouble is I have no idea if it's pity, or if it's something more.

"There we go, it's beautiful," I say.

The painting of a pink splodge with arms and legs is now pride of place on our fridge. Apparently this is a picture of me. Hollie has taken care to give me a particularly round tummy, almost a perfect circle. What else could I do but praise her, even if the humiliation was burning in my eyes. Hollie, satisfied I liked it, immediately dashed away to play outside with her friend Lucy. Sometimes it depresses me that my five-year-old sister has more friends than I do.

I stand by the window so I can keep an eye on her. She is drawing chalk pictures on the paving slabs outside our house. I hope there are no more images of me. Mum is sat at the table, drinking tea and watching me. She looks more tired than usual.

"Did you get any sleep?" I ask.

"Some." She is rubbing her arms. Dark bruises are dotted across them. She looks like rotting fruit. Her face is so pale and heavy-looking. She's not looking after herself. I just wish I could give her a week off. A month, even.

"How did you do that?"

"I bang myself all the time at work," she says, shaking her head. "It's nothing. I love Hollie's painting. Isn't it pretty?"

I look at it again, the massive round thing. I'm just thankful Lyn didn't see it. He sloped off to the shops before I collected her. "It's meant to be me," I say.

"Well, she's given you a lovely smile," Mum says. "How was your day, anyway?"

The rush of guilt almost takes my breath away. I can't even look at her. What if she can see I've been skiving just by looking at me? How can I justify missing school, when she's working so hard she can barely stand up straight?

"It was fine," I say and then, just because I know this would make her really happy, "I've been invited to a party."

"A party! That's so exciting!" Her eyes brighten immediately; the light inside her has been turned on again. "When is it?"

"Saturday, I think." A dark cloud hovers over me. I swear it's Kez's shadow reminding me not to get my hopes up. "I'm not sure though. I might not go."

"Might not go!" Her eyes are really blazing now. She leans towards me. "Why the hell wouldn't you go? This is the first invite you've had since primary school. Things like this are really important, Jess. It'll help your confidence."

"But I've got nothing to wear," I say lamely.

"I'm sure we can find something. What about that dress you wore for Uncle Ken's wedding?"

"That was years ago. It'll be too small." *And it's really naff. I might as well wear a sign round my neck saying* KILL ME NOW. "I need a tent."

"A tent? Don't be silly," Mum says, but I can see that look on her face, that flicker of *but you are fat aren't you*. "I'll find you something. Come here."

Reluctantly, I trail after her. I can still hear Hollie's yelps of joy from outside and I wish I could join her.

Mum is now in her bedroom. She has the smaller room, painted bright pink by the people who lived here before. "I will sort it one day," she always says, but doesn't. It makes me feel sad, coming in here, seeing her single bed unmade and squashed up against the wall. I remember our old house, with the bigger rooms and nice furniture, Mum and

Dad's kingsize bed with the squishy duvet. Most of the furniture was sold and Mum says we're lucky to be able to afford this place.

She opens up her big white wardrobe. It has chipped paint on the side, exposing darker wood. It looks like decay.

"I have some tops," she says. "Maybe we can have a play around."

Mum is dead skinny, probably a size eight, so I really have no idea why she's doing this. But she pulls out some tops and throws them on the bed. I pick one up. Its black, long-sleeved and low cut. It's actually really nice.

"That'll go well with some jeans," she says.

"My jeans are horrible," I say, feeling rubbish again. But the top is so nice and it looks like it'll fit.

"Maybe we can pick some up on Saturday," she says. "I have a little money saved and there's some sales on."

"But we need money for food," I say, shaking my head. "I'm sure I can find something to match. At least the top looks special."

"Well, as long as you're sure. I want my girl to look good."

"I am," I say, but I'm not. Really I want her to

spend all her money on me. The horrible, nasty part of me wants a whole new wardrobe. I want to feel better.

She sighs and sits herself on the bed. "I know it's been hard. If I could just get some regular money from your dad I could treat you both."

"Oh, Mum!" I pull her into a hug, hearing her gasp as I do so. I can feel her bones as I hold her. She's like a tiny doll. The top is still clasped in my hand. "I still don't get how this ever fit you, though?"

"I wore it when I was pregnant with Hollie," she says, gently easing me away. "It's lovely, isn't it?"

Lovely. A top for a pregnant woman. The perfect top for me.

The skinny girl inside is sobbing once again.

How could anyone fancy me?

Have you looked in the mirror lately? Does she wash? Gross. You better show your face. You fat little freak. Fat. fat. fat. You fat little freak. It'll just make things worse. Please, please we need to talk. Evil. RIP. She dresses like such a freak. Please Fat. Fat. Fat. Gross. and say it. It's fine, honest. Yeah, whatever. It's fine, honest. Evil. You fat little freak. LOL Big mistake. LOL. Gross. She dresses like RIP. mirror lately? such a freak. things worse Big mistake. Evil. There's nothing to worry little cow. LOL It'll just make things worse. Have you looked you poor fat little freak. Nxt time I'm calling the police. You're pathetic. please, please. Gross. There's nothing to worry about. On your knees and say it. Gross. You needed to be taught a lesson. You fat little freak. RIP. Yeah, whatever. You poor little cow.

Kez

Marnie is sitting opposite me, pulling her "when will she shut up?" face. I really don't mind Julie going on. She has a loud, friendly voice that makes me want to smile (most of the time). Just as long as she doesn't start on me. I'm just glad I was allowed to stay another night.

"Honestly, Marnie, all I'm saying is you've got to try harder," Julie says as she shuffles across the kitchen, busying herself making coffee.

"Yeah, yeah, I know." Marnie now has her head resting on the kitchen table.

"I just hate calls from the school. You know that. Your Head of Year seems pretty concerned. Says you have so much potential."

More than me, that's for sure. I wonder if they've tried to call home. I think Mum only gave them her number. God knows what would happen if Dad was ever contacted. I shift in my seat at the thought.

"I'm just asking you to try harder, that's all. You don't want to end up like me, do you?" She gestures at her skinny, bronzed body. "Five nights in a pub and trying to run an Avon catalogue. Hardly a shining example of success, am I?"

"You do OK," Marnie mumbles.

"But you could do *better*!" Julie's eyes flicker over to me and I swear I see something there. I don't know what it is. Resentment? Blame? I quickly turn my face and look back at my phone. It's still sitting in my hand, staring at me blankly. No message from Lyn yet. Why hasn't he replied? I sent him a sweet message as soon as I woke up, but still nothing from him.

"What did you two get up to last night anyway?" Julie asks too brightly.

"Nothing," says Marnie, her head still buried.

"We just walked about," I say.

"Not too late I hope. There's nutters about you know. That Terry at number twelve hasn't cleaned his curtains in years. And his eyes point in different directions."

"Hardly makes him a paedo," says Marnie.

"Whatever. You'd soon be running to me if you were buried under a foot of concrete in his back garden."

"Urgh, Mum, you're so sad."

My phone buzzes, the tiny vibrations sending prickles of hope down my spine. He's replied.

This can't carry on. Dad is fuming. You need to come home tonight.

I blink hard at the words. I can feel the curling fist of panic gripping my stomach.

I can't face him.

I send the message before I've even had a chance to consider it. I can picture her at home, somewhere quiet and hidden like the downstairs loo, reading my reply. Hoping I can do what she wants. She sends back her reply.

You have to. We need to get things back to normal. Please.

It's the please that kills me, the further tug in my gut. I know she's probably crying, mentally pleading with me to make things better. But how can I go home, not knowing what I'm going to face? How can I look him in the eye and pretend everything is OK?

"Are you OK, sweetie?" Julie's beady eyes are on me. She never misses anything. Marnie is still buried in her own arms. Sometimes I think she would miss an atomic bomb if it were to go off.

"I'm fine," I say, as I press delete on the message.

Walking into the tutor room is like walking into to a hive of mad, frantic bees. The noise is just crazy. Several of the boys are sat at the back, shouting about some pathetic football game last night. Rosie and Jade are busy doing their make-up. The nerds, who I can't even be bothered to remember to name, are catching up on their work at the front of the room.

I flop on my seat by the window. It's so grey outside, the weather of a slug – slimy and damp. I stare out at the view of a brick wall, broken up with little bursts of moss. Walls surround everything round here, the school, the shopping parade and the Mac. One great big brick fence. I am being slowly suffocated.

"Kez?"

I look up. Lois is standing next to me. This isn't her tutor room.

"What are you doing here? You'll be late," I say.

Miss Welsh is due in any second. She will scuttle in, as usual, in her crazily high shoes and go on in her fake-positive way about what a "fab day we're all going to have". Yeah, right. . .

"This won't take long." Lois isn't looking at me properly and she keeps licking her lips. I can tell she's worrying about something; she may as well have a great luminous sign above her head.

"Go on, then." I pull my bored face, but if I'm honest, this is far from true. My head hurts and that message from Mum keeps flashing through my mind. Dad has all day to brood about me, which isn't good. I feel queasy with nerves. I just know something will kick off.

"It's just – well." She pulls herself upright and sighs. "It's Jess. I'm worried about her. I saw her just walk right past the school gate."

"So?"

"So? Jess never bunks does she – she's not like that. I'm worried about her, Kez. So is Hannah. You know the two of them used to be mates."

"Worried? About her?" I cough back a laugh. "You're kidding, aren't you? She's big enough to look after herself – literally."

133

"I'm just saying."

"Saying what exactly?" I can actually see Dad's face in my head, his glaring eyes. I imagine him at home, turning up his music, pacing the room. The pain is right behind my eyes now, piercing. "What do you want me to do, Lois? Chase after her? Bring her back in?"

"People might notice, though," Lois hisses, leaning towards me. "Hannah and that are already saying how out of order we're being. She says it's gone too far."

"So you listen to Hannah now? Miss No-personality?"

"That's not fair! Hannah just cares." Lois's cheeks are flushed, she grabs her bag. "This is a total waste of time."

"Yeah, it is."

Lois clutches the strap of her bag and leans in right close to me. I can see little flecks of green in her eyes, the small mole above her lip.

"You might not be so smug if Jess reports you," she says. "You shouldn't keep on at her. You don't know what damage you might do."

I watch as she strides out of room. She looks taller.

You don't know what damage you might do. . .

The picture in my head has changed now. To Mum and her swollen, purple face.

I smash my fist against the wall, crying out with pain.

And then I follow Lois out of the room, trying to block out the whispers around me.

"We're just concerned, Keren."

Mr Booth has one of those annoying voices, really drony. He is sat back in his chair, with his hands locked together in front of him. His old, wrinkled face is trying to look concerned but I can see his attention keeps being distracted towards the various emails that keep pinging up on his screen. Being a Head of Year can't be much fun.

"Why? There's nothing wrong," I say, ignoring the pain in my hand.

"You punched a wall, Keren. I hardly think that's nothing. What made you do that?"

"I was just wound up."

"You must've been. It must be sore. After this you need to go to the medical room to get it checked."

"I can move my fingers," I tell him. "It's fine."

"I've been told you were talking to Lois Dobbs

just before. You two are usually friends, aren't you? Do you need me to talk to her?"

I keep staring up at his bald head. It's shining in the light. I can see dry flecks of skin on it. I wonder if he still has to shampoo it. He rubs his nose, still watching me, knocking his glasses off-centre. He looks even weirder now.

"Keren, if you talk to me I can help."

"I'm fine. I don't need your help."

The seat is hard and is making me want to fidget, but I stay still. I want to look calm and in control. My hand remains in my lap, hidden by my coat. I try and ignore the throbbing; at least it's taken my mind off my head.

"I think I should ring your mum, Keren."

"You don't need to ring my mum." I stare at him, willing him to shut up. "I'll show her when I get home."

"It's a safeguarding issue, Keren; the school has a duty to make your parents aware of any concerns."

Why does he keep repeating my name? I really want to scream at him to shut up. Every muscle in me is tightening up. I think I might snap right here in front of him. I look at his bald head again and imagine little pieces of me splattered all over it.

Was I always this angry?

"Just tell me why you did it." He has his pen poised on a piece of paper. The clock is ticking. He obviously wants an answer from me. Something he can scribble down and stuff safely away in my file.

"Lois just pissed me off," I say finally. "She made a comment about my boyfriend. It's nothing. I overreacted. It's fine now, really."

Better they think that, than start asking questions about Jess. Or even worse, my family.

"And your boyfriend is. . . ?" He looks confused. I guess they have a problem with that too.

"Lyn, Lyndon Roberts in Year Eleven."

He nods. Makes the connection. A small frown appears. "Ah, I see. Well, I will have to make your parents aware of that fact too, Keren."

"Do whatever you like, sir," I say.

I pick up my bag and leave.

I don't usually walk home on my own. It's just not what I do. But with Lyn still not answering my texts (and no there was no sign of him at school) and with Marnie at drama rehearsals, I have no other choice.

I walk the long way because I can't face home yet. I know a call would have been made. I know

Dad will be even more wound up. The heaviness in my legs seems even worse now, it's like I'm wading through sludge.

I'm drawn to the Mac like I always am. The marked brick walls and torn chain-link fences are so familiar to me. The burnt-out car that has been sitting in the pub car park for over a month now. The community church with its huge "trying to be welcoming" noticeboard. The primary school with the bright yellow broken gate and stained concrete walls.

The houses are thin, grey and tired. The gardens surrounded by walls, front and back. Everyone seems penned in, shut away. Little patches of yellow grass sit in the middle of each block of housing – Lyn calls them the "dog-crap patches" and usually they are covered in litter and poo, or discarded kids' toys.

But of course everything is overshadowed by the looming tower blocks. Dad calls them "unsightly". Says they should be "knocked down" as they make the whole town look cheap and nasty. I don't know who Dad thinks he is, really. I guess it was different in the days when he used to put on a suit and drive to work in his nice car. I think he thought he was above everyone else then. Trouble is, even though he's not worn his suit for years – even though he spends most days on the sofa – he still thinks he's different.

Personally, I don't mind the towers. They skim the sky, far and reaching. They look like they're in charge of the place. They are the Estate.

Jess lives here, in one of these shoebox flats. I know because I've seen her shuffling around, trying to avoid us. Marnie says her mum has a really nasty job cleaning bogs in a club in town. Apparently she's out every night. I guess that must be hard for them.

I wonder if I'll see her. If I do, what would I say? Am I sorry? Has this gone too far?

I start walking away, towards the park. I feel cluttered, like I want to empty everything out of me and start again. I don't remember ever feeling this tired or confused before.

I hear the voices first, sharp laughter coming from the main path out of the park. I carry on walking towards it. Whoever it is sounds really happy.

And then I see them.

Both of them.

It's like everything inside me has just been sucked away. I have to keep looking just to make sure I'm getting it right. But of course there's little doubt. I know it's him. Lyn. And how could I miss her?

They're walking together. Him and Jess. They are talking and laughing and, Jesus, is his hand touching her waist? It is! He's touching her!

I think I want to be sick.

I think I actually want to kill her now.

"You bitch," I hiss under my breath, before slipping away, my hand reaching for my phone, preparing to call Marnie.

I stay with Marnie for as long as I can, but in the end I know I have to go home. I can't keep hiding away.

I'm so wound up, so on edge that I walk into the house without thinking too much. The whole thing with Lyn and that stig Jess is still replaying in my head like a nasty dream. The front door shuts loudly behind me before I even realize where I am.

I slip my bag on to the floor by the wall and carefully place my keys in the small bowl on the side table. There's a chance of course that he didn't hear me. He might even be asleep. With any luck I can still escape unnoticed.

Creeping past an open door in your own house must be the saddest, most tragic thing that anyone ever has to do. I seem to be making a regular habit of it. I hold my breath. I tense up. I just pray with every fibre of me that he doesn't hear me. But of course, he does.

"Keren. Come in here, please." His voice is cool and controlled. I freeze on the spot. I can't move. It's like when we used to play musical statues as kids, except this time there's no fun-size Mars bar at the end.

"Keren. Come here, please." The voice is louder now, more brittle.

I go in. I try and act casual, because what's the point of being anything else? I keep my face calm, even though the icy feeling of dread is eating me up inside. I can do this. He will not bring me down.

He is sitting there facing me, perched on the edge of the seat in an upright, awkward position. Mum is sat opposite on the smaller sofa. She's facing away, scribbling notes on a notepad. Probably her shopping list or something equally dull. Why won't she look at me?

And then I see the plate on the coffee table. Sausage and mash. I can see the gravy has congealed around them like a muddy jelly. The sausages look grey and thick with cooling fat. The knife and fork are sat beside them like silent soldiers.

"Your dinner was three hours ago," Dad says, still staring at me.

"I know. I'm sorry. I was held up."

"I don't want to hear that," he says, his lip curling. "Your dinner was cooked for you three hours ago. You should've had the decency to come back for it."

I keep my voice neutral; my words come out slow and measured. "Like I said, I was held up. I'm sorry. What else can I do now? I can't rewind time."

"What else can you do?" His eyes are properly glinting now. He starts to laugh, a manic, nasty laugh that cuts right through me. "Did you hear this, Mel? She wants to know what else she can do . . . WELL YOU COULD GET HOME ON TIME FOR A START! SHOW US A BIT OF BLOODY RESPECT!"

His hand slams the table, I see Mum flinch but she still keeps her eyes lowered. I swear she's mumbling something under her breath. I don't move a muscle. I don't want to give him the satisfaction.

"And now, you will eat that dinner."

"Er, you're kidding me."

"Er, no! I'm not. You are going to eat that dinner. Every last mouthful."

I look at it again, the cold mess. I don't like

sausages much at the best of times. "Can I at least heat it in the microwave?"

"No."

"But I might get a bug or something. This is rank. Mum – aren't you going to say something?" I plead.

"Just do as he says," she whispers, still with her head bent. "It won't kill you."

"No." I can feel the anger snaking up me again. Everything – him, Jess, Lyn – it's all too much. I don't have to stand for this. "This is out of order. I'm not doing it."

"Oh yes you are."

He grabs my head before I'm even aware of what he's doing, gripping my hair tightly and forcing me forwards. I try and fight back, but it's useless, his anger makes him ten times stronger. My whole body is being pushed. I can see the dinner coming towards me, one last pathetic look before his whole weight shoves my face into it.

He keeps hold of my hair and moves my head back and forth into the cold, stinky food. All I can feel is mush.

"Eat it," he hisses into my ear.

I keep my mouth clamped shut. He's not going to win.

"Eat it!"

He moves my head faster now. Cold, plastic-tasting meat is forced into my mouth. Mash like lumpy milk goes up my nose, slips down my throat. I'm going to choke. I gag and then I manage to scream. I use my elbows to force him away.

Finally, he lets go and I fall to the floor, dinner dripping off me. My scalp is throbbing. Dad is panting behind me. Mum is sobbing.

"You needed to be taught a lesson," he hisses, before storming out the room. The door slams.

I wipe my face, letting a great lump of potato fall on the carpet. I hope it stains.

I look at my mum and I could scream at her. I didn't cry once and I'm not going to.

I'll never be like her.

Never.

Kez Walker: BIG changes. I'm not bein made a mug of again. . .;o(

3 hours ago.

Like   Comment   Share

Marnie: You OK babe?

Kez: NO!

Marnie: Dont worry. We'll sort it

Kez: Yeah. We better. Not bein made a fool of by anyone!

Lois: I'm sorry if ur still mad at me . . . I just had 2 say somethin

Kez: Not mad at u, but things changed. The stig is winding me up. And others

Lois: Really? Tell me 2

Kez: Will do

Lyn: You ok?

Kez: We need to talk.

Lyn: Ok. C u tomorro.

Friday

You poor little cow. She offends my eyes. Big mistake. On your knees and say it. This is not over. Please, please, please. Have you looked in the mirror lately? There's nothing to worry. This is not over. We need to talk. Evil. Gross. LOL. Does she wash? Evil. Does she Evil. This is not over. We need to talk so... Fat. poor little cow You needed to please, please be taught a please. Evil. Gross. lesson. It's fine. You're pathetic. Fat. worry about police. On your knees and honest. Evil. There's nothing to calling the police. say it. Gross and Nxt time I'm your fat little freak. Fat. Fat. Fat. RIP. Evil. You fat Big mistake. Gross. You needed to be taught a lesson. It'll just make things wo Fat. Fat. Fat. Have you looked in the mirror lately? It's fine, honest. RIP.

Jess

"Why don't we ever see Dad now?"

Hollie is walking slowly today, dragging her bag along the floor, making a nasty scraping sound. She's been whining all morning. I had to literally pull her out of bed this morning and then she just laid herself on the floor in a hot, crying lump. It's impossible to love her when she's like this, it would be like loving a creation from a horror film.

"He's busy," I say.

"Doing what? I want to see him. I made him a picture."

"Working, I think."

I hate lying to her. I want to take her grubby hand in mine and march her over to number 32, Beaches Rise and knock on the door. *There you go, there's our dad. He actually lives ten minutes away, he just can't be bothered to see us. Oh, ignore the crying in the other room — that's his*

149

other kid, your little brother or sister. Go on, say hello. . .

"But Tyler's daddy works and he still sees him."

Tyler is Hollie's best friend. The two of them usually walk round the playground holding hands, or searching for bugs together in the mud. A bit like someone I used to know. . .

"I don't know, Hollie, it's complicated."

That's what Mum always says when she wants to fob me off, so it sounds like the right thing to say in this situation. Hollie seems satisfied; she nods and finally decides to skip ahead of me. This is good as it leaves me to wallow in my own worries, these being:

1) Going back into school, after bunking, with no note to explain why.
2) Going back into school and facing Kez again.
3) Going back into school and facing PE, with no note to excuse me from it.

I'm particularly annoyed about 3) as I'd asked Mum last night to get me away from the HELL that is PE but she forgot. So now I'm going to be subject to the torture of undressing in front of the other skinny, perfect girls and then made to run around in shorts that are far too small for me. It's not as though the PE teachers are even that horrible. Miss Gregory is sweet, blonde and perky with lovely long legs and a bright, barky voice that bounces through the gym. Miss Frazer, who's much older but even more muscular, even tries to encourage me, tells me I'd make a good hockey player if I'd let my confidence issues go. It's just neither of them really understand how hard PE is for someone like me. It's not just the session itself. It's the before and after. The constant humiliation.

It wouldn't be so bad if I didn't wobble. It wouldn't be so bad if my skin wasn't such a ghostly white, marked only by the bluish stains of bruises and veins that stand out like tattoos.

It wouldn't be so bad if it were just me in the room.

"Jess! Jess!"

Hollie is tugging on my arm. We are at the gate on the school. Throngs of children are pushing their way through.

"You stopped," she says. "Why did you stop?"

She is looking at me so confused. I had no idea I had just been standing there. "I'm sorry," I say, grabbing her hand, "let's go."

"You looked sad. Like Mum does."

I stare down at her wide eyes. Sometimes I forget just how small she is. She must get so scared too.

"I'm not sad," I say, as firmly as I can. "I'm not sad at all."

I march her into school, forcing all the worries into the back of my mind.

Silly worries. Not important.

It will be OK. It has to be.

"So this Lyn. . . What sort of name is that anyway?" Phillip is looking particularly confused. He's studying me like I'm some kind of weird insect that he's just found on the chair. It's a bit unnerving.

"It's short for Lyndon."

"Oh. I see. So, this Lyn, he's decided to invite you to his party and he just happens to be dating the girl you hate the most?" Phillip's nose wrinkles. "Interesting."

"I guess, when you put it like that; but we used to be friends, good ones."

Phillip is sitting in the library, working on his maths project. He looks more relaxed today. I'm not sure why. Maybe it's because he's allowed his hair to fluff out a little. It kind of suits him.

"I take it you're going?" he says, not looking at

me now as he adds more lines. He is so careful with each one.

"Well, I said I was, but I wasn't really thinking then. Now I'm not so sure."

"Why?" Phillip waves his ruler at me. "The host has invited you. It would be rude not to go, surely?"

"Duh! Kez will be there. And Marnie! Or have you forgotten that? If they see me there, they will tear me to pieces. I'm sure Lyn doesn't want his living room redecorated with my body parts."

Phillip seems to be considering this. His forehead wrinkles and he looks like he's going into some kind of trance. "But surely she wouldn't do anything in front of Lyn?"

"Why not?"

"Because that would make her look bad in front of him. If she finds out he invited you, she has to respect that or risk upsetting him. You're his friend; surely she has to begin to recognize that?"

"I guess."

"So I'm thinking it would be in her best interests to be nice to you. Or at least tolerate you." Phillip frowns at me. "Which I admit is hard to do at the best of times."

"What do you mean?" I say, slightly thrown by this.

"Well, look at you, all slumped over like a defeated maggot. Sit up. Smile. Relax."

I stare at him, unable to speak for a moment. But he just flaps his ruler again at me. He's smiling and I know he's not meaning to sound harsh, his words can just be a bit blunt sometimes. I find myself sitting upright.

"That's better. Much better," he grins. "I'm good at this."

"Maybe. But I'm still not sure Kez will be so happy to leave me alone."

"You might be surprised. My mum always says that the slowest of worms can turn."

I shake my head. "I don't think she's capable of that."

"This could actually be your perfect revenge."

"How's that?"

Phillip is smiling now; I think he's actually enjoying this. "Because if you do make her lose control with you, she'll end up losing her boyfriend."

I can't help grinning back. "Thanks. For that I'll forgive you calling me a maggot."

Phillip just shrugs and goes backs to his lines. "I think you'll find they're actually extremely useful creatures."

I can't help loving him just a little bit.

*

In PE all I want to do is hide.

The benches are cold and unforgiving, as is the hard, heavily marked floor. And the girls are always louder and crueller in this room. The enclosed, windowless walls seem to bring out the worst in them.

I usually sit in the same place, in the corner, far away from the mirrors. The pretty girls crowd there, and Kez and Marnie are normally at the front. They do their hair before PE and their make-up after. The glass is marked with specks of mascara and globs of lipstick. I would like to go over and brush my own hair, make sure it's all in place, but I don't want to be anywhere near them. So instead I sit here and wonder if it's possible to blend into the beige of the wall.

If only I was a maggot. No one would see me then.

Getting dressed is the worst bit. I've tried both ways, slow and drawn-out and fast and over with. Both have their pitfalls. Slow means I have control. I make sure some item of clothing is draped over my flabbier parts, disguising the flaws – but this also means I'm often the last to be ready. Which leaves them looking at me, smirking. Fast means I go for it and can be done before anyone else, but I have less control and there's always the risk that they catch a look at my exposed belly or wobbly thighs.

Today I chose fast and of course today I get spotted.

"Errgh. Honestly, your belly is so huge. I swear it's getting bigger."

Kez is standing directly in front of me. She's already half changed, standing in just her shorts and bra. It's like she wants to taunt me with her beautiful, lean body. I can't help staring at her stomach; it's so firm and pink, like plastic.

"What are you looking at?" She moves forward now, swaggering. She points at herself. "Oh my God, Jess, are you copping a look at my boobs?"

"No . . . I . . ." My cheeks are burning now. I can see she's caught everyone's attention, the whole room is quiet. I pray for Miss Gregory to come back in. She's usually here supervising, but went out a few minutes ago to check on another student.

"You were. I saw you. So not only are you a fat freak, you're also a lesbo!" She smiles sweetly at me. "Well, I guess it must be tough. It's not like any fella's going to fancy you."

I turn away. Dig around in my bag for my top. I just want to cover myself up. I can actually feel the weight of my flab pulling me down. My whole body is rigid and cold. I can hear Marnie giggling behind me.

"Aren't you going to say anything?" Marnie says. "You're not even trying to deny it."

I see Phillip in my head; I try to imagine what he would do. "I shouldn't have to deny anything," I say as calmly as I can, pulling the top over my head. For a brief second, in the darkness, I shut my eyes and pray for this to end.

"Well, that just proves it then," Marnie says, smug now. "If someone said that to me I would punch them. Hard."

"I'm not you," I say, my voice wobbling. "But I'm not a lesbian either."

Kez's face is colder than ever, like it's been carved out of ice. I always thought she was so beautiful, but up close like this all I can see are hard lines and heavy make-up. "You were checking me out. I saw you. And you've been sniffing around me and my man. It all makes sense now, you sad little freak."

"I've not been sniffing around anyone. I avoid you. And Lyn came to me. We're old friends."

Kez's face freezes. Her eyes are piercing into me now. She swallows hard. "What did you say?"

"I said Lyn came to me." I'm not sure where this tone in my voice has come from. I find myself standing taller, like Phillip told me to do. "I've not been sniffing around. Lyn and me have been talking. We just get on; we always have. We met up yesterday by chance. Ask him."

She's still staring, but I can see something in her shift. Doubt? Worry?

"And he's invited me tomorrow night. He wants me to come," I add softly.

"You what?"

"Lyn wants me at the party."

I hear a movement then. Hannah has pushed her way forward. "Oi! Kez, leave it!" she says. But Kez is not listening.

"Why would he want you there?" she hisses.

I don't answer. How can I? I don't know the answer myself.

She moves so quickly I don't have time to react. I just feel the burning, blistering pain as her hand strikes my skin.

"You bitch!" she screams.

She slaps me again and her long nails claw at my face.

Miss Gregory walks in to the girls whooping and screeching, expecting a fight. She pulls Kez away from me, still yelling, as I sink back on the bench. I feel so heavy.

The pain in my cheek isn't bothering me. It's the look in Kez's eyes as she's led away.

If she hated me before, she absolutely loathes me now.

"I can't believe this happened in school. She's actually left a mark on your skin!"

Mum grabs my face and turns it sharply towards her. I flinch. "It's nothing. It's fine, honest."

"It's not fine. It's far from fine." She drops her hand and moves away from me. "I'm ringing the school. This can't happen. It's not right."

"It was dealt with. Please, Mum, don't make a fuss. It'll just make things worse."

"How was it dealt with?"

"I said it was nothing. I told the teacher I wound the girl up. I don't want it to go further."

She stops and turns. "This is the bully, isn't it? The one you were worried about before?"

I half shrug. I'm so tired. I don't want this right now. I just want to lie on my bed with the duvet over my head. Read a book. Forget about the whole stupid day.

Mum rubs her face. "I'm so sorry, Jess. I should've listened before. I just figured it was girls saying stuff. You know, stupid things. I didn't think it would ever get physical."

"And now they've hit me, so that makes it worse?" I say quietly.

"No. Of course not." She sounds confused. She sits next to me on the sofa. I look down at her long fingers that are fiddling with her skirt hem, at her exposed white legs, with bulging veins like tiny worms snaking up her calves. Her feet are long and bony and the toes bend out of shape. I wonder if it's because she walks so much.

"What are you staring at?" she asks, drawing her feet back against the sofa. "I know they look horrible. I've always had disgusting feet."

I remember Kez accusing me of staring at her boobs and I can feel the shame burn in my cheeks.

"I wasn't staring," I whisper.

"Jess, what on earth is wrong?" She pulls me towards her. The scent of her is so familiar; I bury my head in her top, rubbing my cheek against the rough material. She starts stroking my head, slow soft strokes and I close my eyes.

"It will get better. You just need to rise above them," she mumbles into my hair.

"They hate me."

"How could they possibly hate you? You're beautiful. They must be jealous."

I pull myself away from her, rub my tear-streaked face. Is she even seeing me properly? "You are kidding right? I'm disgusting."

Her face pales. "Don't say that, Jess. It's not true."

"I'm fat, clumsy and ugly. And now they're saying I'm a lesbian too."

"Who's saying this?"

"It doesn't matter. I'm not telling you because I don't want it getting worse."

Mum sighs. Her whole body seems to deflate. "I just want to help, Jess."

"I don't want your help," I say flatly. "I told the school the same. I said it was nothing. It's not worth the grief if I make more fuss."

"But, Jess, you can't let these stupid girls get to you. Do you really believe they're right?"

I jump up. I swear my whole body wobbles as I do so. "Just look at me. Of course they're right."

Mum sits there for a few seconds, staring at me. Then she stands up and takes my arm, still not saying anything. She leads me down the hall, past the bedroom where Hollie is quietly playing and into the bathroom. She stands me in front of the mirror.

"Look in there and tell me what you see," she says.

I stare back at the pink blob. The shapeless, lardy, formless mass that fills the entire glass. I want to put my fist through it. "I see a fat lump," I say.

"I see beautiful clear skin. Bright, large green eyes. Long eyelashes. Full lips. And the most lovely, long dark hair with a natural wave that I would kill for." Mum squeezes her face next to me, so that both our images are projected side by side. "I've always hated my horrible thin lips, my piggy eyes and wishy-washy hair – luckily, you take after your dad."

"A dad that hates me too," I whisper.

"He doesn't hate you. He's just . . . well, he's just a bit useless." She kisses my cheek. "And I have been a bit lately, too. I'm sorry. Things will get easier soon, I promise."

"I just want to speak to him. I don't understand why he's cut us off like this."

"Well, maybe you could try calling him?" Mum says. "I'm not promising anything – he never returns my calls – but if you want to try?"

"I would like to," I say, a rush of fear and

excitement is hitting me at once. I didn't think she'd be so nice about it.

"I just hope this makes you feel a better."

"A bit. But I'm still fat."

"You're a little overweight. But it's nothing major and if you're so worried about it, we can look at helping you. We can get some healthy food in? Maybe we could do a class together, or go running. It might be fun, you never know."

I keep looking at our two faces. Mum's tired, pale face seems so thin next to mine. I still look like an elephant. But I guess she is right about my eyes, they are quite big.

"Rise above it, Jess, don't sink," Mum whispers. "You're more beautiful than you ever imagine."

Later, before I go to bed, I log on to the internet. I'm surprised to see a private message waiting for me. I never get those. When I see it's from Lyn, I'm even more amazed.

I click it open.

Hey Jess

I heard what happened today. It's not cool. I've finished with Kez so she knows the score.

Hope you're still coming tomorrow night? Really wanna c u.

Keep smiling.

Lyn x

I write my reply straight away, my heart beating fast.

Hi

I'll be there. Looking forward to it.

Sorry about you and Kez.

J

This is the first time a guy's ever sent me a message – and this guy is really, really fit. On top of that, he's ended things with Kez, which must mean she won't be at the party tomorrow. Mustn't it?

Minutes later another private message pops up. I open it, my heart pumping with excitement. Except this time it's not Lyn.

Looking forward to seeing u at the party tomorrow – you little fat freak. And if you don't go, I'll get you another time, so you better show ur ugly face.

You mess with my life and you'll regret it.

It's payback time.

K

I shut down the computer. I cannot bear to read it again. This nightmare is just getting a whole lot worse and I don't even know what to do about it.

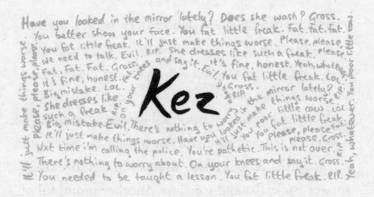

Have you looked in the mirror lately? Does she wash? Gross. You better show your face. You fat little freak. Fat. fat. fat. You fat little freak. It'll just make things worse. Please, please, we need to talk. Evil. RIP. She dresses like such a freak. Please, Fat. Fat. Gross. and say it. It's fine, honest. Yeah, whatever. It's fine, honest. Evil. You fat little freak. Lol. Big mistake. Lol. Gross. She dresses like the mirror lately? such a freak. make things worse? Big mistake. Evil. There's nothing to worry. little cow. Lol. It'll just make things worse. Have you fat little freak. Nxt time i'm calling the police. You're pathetic. This is not over. There's nothing to worry about. On your knees and say it. Gross. You needed to be taught a lesson. You fat little freak. RIP.

Kez

Is it possible to hate someone any more than you already do? I don't think so, I really don't. I think my hate level is totally maxed out. I was told that there is a fine line between love and hate. Does that mean I'm going to start loving him again? Because I'm really not sure I can.

I'm sitting opposite him, Dad, only because Mum snuck into my room early and begged me. Told me that she needed one more morning of being normal. Can't she see this is all a big joke? I feel like we're putting on a play for someone else's benefit. I keep expecting to turn around and see the audience sitting there, bags of popcorn on their laps, swallowing up our lies.

Dad is eating his toast really slowly, taking effort with each bite. The newspaper is open in front of him but he's not looking at it. He's watching me. I eat my cornflakes carefully and deliberately. I don't want to talk. I don't want anything to do with him. At the sink Mum is keeping herself busy washing things; I see that she has been washing the same mug for five minutes now – that must be some kind of record.

"What lessons have you got today?" he asks.

"English. Art. Music. Maths. PE." I fire each answer back, flat and toneless. Another mouthful of soggy slush enters my mouth. I think I'm losing my sense of taste, everything seems like cardboard.

"I hope you're up to date with your homework."

I think of my science and almost blush. My English is well overdue too, but I can't get on with romantic books. "I am," I say instead.

He takes a slug of coffee, still watching me. "Mum says you've been hanging around with the kids on the Estate."

I look over at Mum; her arms are working furiously in the suds. I didn't even know she cared where I'd been. I really don't see what this has to do with anything.

"I think you should reconsider your friendship groups. I've noticed a marked change in your behaviour of late."

You've noticed a marked change in my behaviour since

167

you've started smashing the place up more, Dad. Using
Mum as a punching bag. Am I next?

Of course, I don't say this, I just sit there chewing.
I can't seem able to swallow my mouthful.

"Whatever happened to that other girl you used
to be with all the time?"

"Lois," Mum chips in helpfully. "I liked her."

"She's still around," I say. "But I like Marnie too."

Dad pulls his newspaper towards him and
carefully folds it and then slowly stands up. He
moves carefully, unwinding like a large snake.

"And like I said, you might want to think carefully
about those friendship groups," he says in his soft,
spiteful manner, "if you want to remain in this house."

He leaves, closing the door quietly behind him.
I finally feel able to swallow the last spoonful of
soggy cereal. It seems to struggle as it slides down
my throat, scratching my insides.

"You can't tell me what to do," I hiss at the closed
door.

Meanwhile Mum continues to wash. It's still the
same cup.

"So what will you do?" Marnie says. She's only
half listening to me. She has her phone out and is

checking her messages again. I know she's hoping Ben will text her about tomorrow night. She's so fixated on him it's kind of painful.

"I dunno. I'm not sure who I wanna deal with first, my dad or Lyn."

It's break and there is actually a gap in the rain that just seems non-stop at the moment. We've taken the opportunity to grab some air outside. Marnie has smuggled in a bag of sweets and we are chewing them greedily.

"But your dad can't stop you seeing me, surely? What have I ever done to him?" I lick the sugar away from my lips. It's the sour stuff and it burns my tongue. I'm not even sure what to tell her. I can hardly say that my dad is an unemployed slob, who thinks he's better than her just because he's not living on the Mac. Even though I can't stand him most of the time, I don't want other people to know what he's like.

"You've not done anything. He's just in a mood. He'll get over it," I say instead.

She nods. "At least you've got a dad. All I know about mine was that he had a bald head and a thick moustache. I just hope I don't take after him."

We both giggle. Marnie swings her legs. "I wouldn't worry about Lyn either. It's not like he's going to be after Jess, is it? Seriously, who'd pick her over you?"

"I saw them together though and they were laughing." I pause, considering it for a minute. "You know, Marnie, she is quite pretty."

"You what? Jess? The stig? We are talking about the same person here?"

"I dunno. If you look at her properly. If she made an effort. She has a pretty face, dead natural."

"Maybe. But she's still fat."

"Yeah, I know. But Lyn might see the other stuff."

Marnie is looking at me like I'm mad. Maybe I am. All I know is that I need a ton of help to get the skin and eyes that Jess has.

"I don't think you have anything to worry about," Marnie says. "But you have to stand up for yourself. You can't let people walk all over you."

Marnie is staring at me, almost challenging me to disagree with her. I can see the hard glint in her eye, the one she always flashes me when she wants me to agree with her.

"Maybe, but she has something about her, that's all I'm saying."

"The day you start believing stuff like that, is the day you're going to start letting people make a mug of you," she says.

I think of Dad. I remember that dinner last night. The gravy in my nostrils, the mash in my hair — if I concentrate hard enough, I can still taste it. Hasn't this happened to me already?

"Do you wanna be known as weak?" she continues. She's pressing my buttons. It's like she can see right inside my head.

No, I don't want to be known as that. I can't. It's bad enough that I allowed it to happen at home.

"No. But what else can I do? I told her to stay away. She's not listening."

"Tell her again, make her listen."

"OK," I nod. "I can do that."

"We have PE next. What better time to make the stig see herself for what she really is. She'll leave Lyn alone then."

I smile back; of course. PE is perfect. I'll get her then.

But as we walk back to lesson and I'm listening to her droning on about Ben again, I can't help wondering why everything suddenly feels so much effort.

Have I stopped caring? Or am I getting too weak to fight?

Like Mum.

She's always in the changing rooms first. I'm not sure why. Does she think she can hide away or something? It's difficult to miss her. She makes it worse by sitting in the corner by herself and doing this real performance when she gets changed. I nudged Marnie as soon as we walked in.

"Look, there she is, not even bothering to cover herself up this time."

Sometimes I've watched her undress while still clothed. It's like she makes a tent within her own clothing. I suppose she thinks if we don't see her flesh we won't know how fat she actually is.

I start stripping off by the mirrors. Marnie is busy slapping on some cream. It's one of Julie's, and Marnie uses it regularly thinking it will keep wrinkles away. I think she has a morbid fear of growing old. I glance at my own face in the glass as I undress. I hate the way I'm looking today; I left in such a rush I didn't get a chance to make myself up properly. I look like a washed-out version of me, all faded and tired.

"Are you feeling OK?" asks Lois, who is on the bench opposite me. She's obviously noticed how rubbish I look.

"I'm fine," I say, pulling on my shorts.

"It's just you look, a bit . . . I don't know . . . sad," she says lamely.

"Sad! I'm not sad!" I say back with false brightness. "But I tell you who *is* sad. . ."

My eyes have fallen on Jess. She's moving faster now. I think she knows I've noticed her. Her thighs are wobbling like lardy jelly. I move nearer to her.

"Honestly, your belly is so huge. I swear it's getting bigger." The words fly out of my mouth, and hit her like a missile. She seems to recoil. Direct hit!

She just continues to stand there, clutching her top against the rolls of her stomach. Her breathing is fast, almost panting. She looks at me in a weird way, sort of up and down and then coming to rest on my breasts. Her eyes remain there and I feel exposed; it's a weird, unnerving feeling. I want to move away from her green-eyed stare.

"What are you looking at? Oh my God, Jess, are you copping a look at my boobs?"

I just want her to stop gawping at me. I say it louder than I actually mean to and now everyone's attention is on me and Jess. The crowd start to move behind me, eager to see what is going to happen next. I hear one of the girls whisper, "Jess is in trouble now." I can't help smiling. I'm back in control.

Jess is stuttering, near tears. She's shaking her head at me, protesting, but I can't really hear what she's saying. Her lips are opening and shutting – saying something – stupid, useless words. All I can do is wonder what she was talking to Lyn about yesterday.

How come you can make him laugh? I can't do that. It's not fair. What do you do with that sweet little mouth of yours?

"You were. I saw you. So not only are you a fat freak, you're also a lesbo!" I say, the rage burning. "Well, I guess it must be tough. It's not like any fella's going to fancy you."

Because you're not having my man. He's not going to fancy you. I won't let him.

Marnie has come over now, forced herself through the crowd. Her face is glowing; she's enjoying this. She goes up to Jess and challenges her, asks her why she's not denying being a lesbian.

". . .I'm not a lesbian either," Jess says.

But I'm angry now. Just looking at her pathetic, wobbly face is winding me up. This must all be an act. I can't believe that anyone who is capable of chatting to Lyn so causally can look so feeble now. She wants everyone to feel sorry for her, I'm sure of it. "You were checking me out. I saw you. And you've been sniffing around me and my man. It all makes sense now, you sad little freak."

"I've not been sniffing around anyone. I avoid you. And Lyn came to me."

It's like everything is going into slow motion around me. All I can hear is my own heartbeat thumping in my ears like a muted drum. "What did you say?"

"I said Lyn came to me." Her voice has changed somehow. She sounds cool and calm. This is winding me up even more. "I've not been sniffing around. Lyn and me have been talking. We just get on. We met up yesterday by chance. Ask him. And he's invited me tomorrow night. He wants me to come," she adds softly.

"You what?" The thumping is louder now. It's nearly deafening me.

"Lyn wants me at the party."

My hand hits her face before I can even think. And again. The stinging in my hand is the fire from my belly. I can feel her skin under my nails.

I want to fly at her, rip those wide, green eyes out, but I'm pulled away before I can lay another finger on her.

"Nice one," Marnie hisses as Miss Gregory appears and heaves me away.

But I feel nothing.

"We meet again."

Mr Booth sits in front of me. Arms folded. It's more serious this time, I can tell by the small frown on his face, by the notepad in his hand, by my file on the desk.

I sit and stare at the window beyond him. It's really raining now, streaking across the glass, even watching it is making me feel cold. My bones feel like ice blocks inside me, heavy and brittle.

"Are you going to tell me why you did it?" he asks.

"Will it make a difference?" I say.

"It might. Maybe I can get my head round what would make a girl strike another for no apparent reason."

"I don't like her."

"That's not a reason, Keren."

I keep staring outside. I imagine I'm standing

there, getting soaked. Would I feel any colder than I do right now?

"I really don't think you realize how serious this is, Keren. I will have to talk to Jess and then the head teacher. And your parents. I turned a blind eye before, but not this time. If it turns out that this was an unprovoked attack, you may end up suspended."

My eyes flick over to his.

Do you know what he'll do me to me if you suspend me? Do you realize just how much worse things are going to get for me right now? Don't do this.

"Is there anything you want to tell me," he says softly, leaning right towards me. "Anything that might help your case?"

"No," I say. "She deserved it."

And she deserves a whole lot more.

All I want to do is talk to Lyn.

I was meant to wait in the back room for Mum to come and collect me from school, but like that was ever going to happen. Luckily, Ms Ralph, the school secretary put in charge of babysitting me, was distracted by a delivery man – and I had an opportunity to slip out of the front unnoticed. It was so simple I almost found myself laughing.

Lyn wasn't in school again today, which was weird. I'm not sure what he's been up to. I can't understand why he's not called me, or at least messaged to tell me what's going on. It feels like I'm not his girlfriend at all. I'm nothing.

I head towards his flat. It's the only place I can think to go. It's still raining hard and I'm wearing a skimpy denim jacket over my school uniform.

Stupid girl, never dressing appropriately.

Dad's words are still tearing through my head. I feel like he's taking up all the remaining space inside my brain. If I squeeze my eyes shut, I can still see that leering face, the accusing glare. Why is he always angry with me? So disappointed? I wish there was a way I could make him happy again, but I don't even know where to start. Everything seems all smashed up now, like a Lego set with the bits scattered everywhere. Someone needs to find us the instructions, tell us how to fix it back up again. But what if the pieces are broken? What if some bits have been lost for ever? Can it ever be the same again?

I'm walking fast, trying to avoid the huge puddles that are forming in the dips of the pavement; muddy beige lakes are swelling up, taking over the entire street. My strides become longer, clumsier. The denim of my coat is heavy and starting to smell a bit like an old dog. My wet hair is glued to my face. I must look such a state. I bet my mascara is streaking too. It's only a cheap one that Marnie lent me.

Hardly anyone is around of course. In this weather, everyone stays safely tucked inside. A bus roars past and I see faces pressed to the window, staring out at me. I want to be with them, I want to be rushing away somewhere – not staggering in the wet. A tall woman with an umbrella barges past me. Her face flashes with disgust as she glances in my direction. I probably look like a washed-up rat, something she'd rather not touch. I'm half tempted to bare my teeth at her, snotty cow.

I keep my head down, praying that Mum and Dad don't pass in the car. If they spot me here, that's it. Game over. Hopefully they will take the back route and knowing Dad they will, he'll want to avoid the traffic.

Knowing Dad... But do you? Now?

I press on. Damp coat clutched round my neck. Shoes now squelching in the small pools around my feet.

The tower block rises above me and this time I view it with a nervous dread. The windows look dark, like blinkered eyes shut against me. The rain has turned the bricks darker, making them more menacing somehow.

Lyn lives in Tower A, diagonally opposite Marnie's. I push open the door. A group of boys are standing by the entrance. I don't even want to look at what they're doing, so I just walk past them. One of them shouts something. I block it out, I'm not interested.

I consider the lift. It's waiting there and it is working – but then I think of the group behind me. I can still hear them laughing. I imagine them pushing into the lift behind me. I'm wet, cold and looking disgusting and now I feel so exposed. I quickly take the stairs to save any further hesitation.

Seventeen floors is hard. After eight I'm puffing heavily. I have to take a break and lean against the window. I consider digging out my phone, telling Lyn I'm here, but something holds me back. I stare instead out of the yellowing glass. My parents will be at the school by now. They'll be told about Jess. I know I won't be able to go home again tonight. I open my bag and pull out my compact mirror. Immediately I see black rings beneath my eyes. I look like an emo who's been in a fight. I find some tissues buried at the bottom and rub away as much as I can. I look plainer now, empty.

I take the remaining stairs more slowly. I'm not even sure what I'm going to say to Lyn when I see him. At the sixteenth floor I almost turn back, wondering what the hell I'm doing chasing after him anyway, but my stupid feet keep leading me up.

His door is there as I turn the corner. Bright green, the paint slightly chipped around the frame. No doorbell, so I have to bang on the wood, which I do before I can stop myself. It comes out louder than I mean to, making me sound impatient and cross.

Lyn opens the door. He takes a few seconds to register who it is.

"Kez. What are you doing here?"

"I wanted to see you."

He stands there for a moment, just looking at me. Then he shrugs and opens the door further. He looks really stiff and unfriendly.

I step into his flat. It's bigger than I imagined, but very dark. I wonder if he has all the lights turned off and if so, why. The hall is long and shadowy. The radiator is covered with clothes. He leads me into the room at the far end, the living room. It's large with a huge window at the far side. I'm surprised by the lack of furniture and "stuff", though. Just a sofa and chair, a TV and some boxes stacked up in the corner. No bookshelves. No pictures. No cushions.

"It's just me and my dad," he says, by way of explanation.

"I didn't realize," I say. "Is your mum away?"

The *away* hangs between us, a stupid thing to say. He frowns at me. "No. She left when I was a baby. I don't know where she is."

"I'm sorry, I didn't know."

"You didn't ask," he says flatly.

Yeah, well, you don't ask stuff about me either. . .

I stare at him. This is awkward. He's just standing there, arms folded. He's not offering me a drink, asking me anything. He doesn't want me here, it's obvious.

"I heard about you this afternoon," he says suddenly.

"What? What did you hear?"

"I heard you slapped Jess. Had a go at her for nothing. Was pretty nasty actually."

"Who told you?" I hiss. I can imagine Jess straight on the phone to him, bleating away, begging him to sort it all out for her.

"It doesn't matter." He sighs. "But to be honest I'm not interested in this. I don't want some jealous girlfriend beating up people I'm friendly with. I don't want to be with someone so . . . well, so vicious."

"You shouldn't be friendly with the likes of her."

His eyes spark. "I shouldn't what? Are you telling me what I can and can't do now?"

"No! I'm just saying; she's a complete loser."

Lyn laughs. It's a soft, unforgiving laugh. I've heard it before, from another man. I think part of me is dying.

"The only loser is you, Kez; take a look in the mirror sometime. I think you should go. I really don't want to see you right now."

"Are you saying. . .?"

"I'm saying I don't want to be with you any more. I'm sorry, Kez. I just think it's better this way."

Then he turns and walks away from me.

I leave with tears of anger streaming down my face. A fire rages inside me, burning.

This is not over.

I will not let her win.

Kez Walker: Let the fun and games begin. . .

58 minutes ago.

Like   Comment   Share

Marnie: Lol. Someone is sooooo wound up right now. Just glad ur with me babe!

Lois: U OK?

Kez: NO!! But I will be

Marnie: We are plotting – heeee heeee

Kez: STIG ATTACK!

Lois: Oh I see

Hannah: Hasnt this gone on 2 long?

Marnie: Butt out Hannah

Hannah: I'm only saying

Kez: Yeah, well you don't know all the facts. You will soon

Hannah: I know most of the facts. It was me that told Lyn about today btw

Kez: Big mistake Hannah

Hannah: Whatever. This is getting boring

Marnie: Far from it. Things are going to get v. interestin

Saturday

You poor little cow. She offends my eyes. Big mistake.
On your knees and say it. This is not over. Please, please, please.
face. RIP. looked in the mirror lately? There's nothing to worry
Have you looked in the mirror lately? There's nothing to worry
This is not over. We need to talk. LoL Evil. Gross. LoL
Does she wash? Evil. Does she wash? This is not over.
We need to talk so over. Does she Fat. Poor little cow
You needed to LoL please, please,
be taught a please. Evil. Gross.
lesson. It's fine, You're pathetic. Fat. worry about. police.
on your knees and honest. There's nothing calling the freak.
say it. Gross and Evil. Next time you fat little freak.
Fat. Fat. fat. RIP. Big mistake. Gross.
You needed to be taught a lesson. It'll just make things wo
Have you looked in the mirror lately? It's fine, honest. RIP.

Jess

So I'm not going tonight, that's that decided. I've
just texted Hannah to tell her, as she was going to
walk over with me. It's safer to stay away. I can't
face Kez on a normal day, let alone when she's even
more wound up. Even the thought of those ice-cold
eyes are enough to send me into a panic.

"Why do you look so sad again?" Hollie asks
me, as we walk over to the park. We usually spend
Saturday mornings there, it gives Mum a chance to
get some rest. At least today is a bit brighter. Hollie
is kicking at every bit of litter she sees. She loves
jumping on drink cans and hearing the metallic
crunching sound they make. Sometimes a dribble of
liquid will splash out, leaving sticky puddles.

"I'm not sad," I lie. Every step is heavy. I wonder
if other people are looking at me and seeing a fat
girl. A huge, disgusting girl. I've put on my biggest

coat, the one that completely swamps me. Mum hates it, says I look like an old granny in it. But it has no shape, so it suits me.

"I heard you crying in bed," Hollie says, picking up a dry old leaf and handing it to me. "Look, this is the shape of a triangle."

"Sometimes I find things hard. But everyone cries, Hollie, even you."

"I cry when I hurt myself and when Ben Langdon took my favourite pencil. He's the nastiest boy in my class."

"I have a nasty person in school too. She's not very nice to me," I say. I scrunch up the leaf without thinking and throw it on the ground.

"You should tell a teacher. They'll take her pencil away," Hollie says, nodding softly to herself like she's just solved all of my problems. I ruffle her hair; it's like fine cotton under my fingers.

I smile at her, wondering what I'd do without her. My sunshine.

"You should tell Mum. Mum makes things better."

"Maybe, Hollie. Maybe that's what I should do."

Hollie skips ahead, happy that she's sorted me out. I watch as she runs through the gate, straight over to the swings where she always goes. She'd stay on them all day if she could – rocking back and forth. I try and ignore the bench where I sat with Lyn. I wonder for a brief second how his dad is. I hope everything is OK; he seemed so worried. I feel a tug inside and wish I could be with Lyn again.

But even if he liked me, he'd soon go off me if he saw Kez laying into me. Telling everyone the truth, about what a freak I really am.

No one could fancy me.

I hover by the fence, leaning against the splintered wood. In my pocket is the number, scribbled on a torn bit of newspaper. Mum scrawled it down this morning, pressed it into my hand and begged me not to raise my hopes. My fingers dip in now and reach for the folded edge. I draw it out. The digits that could bring me in contact with Dad again. Would he be pleased to hear from me? Three years of no contact; surely he must have missed us a bit?

Hollie is waving to me as I punch out the number on my phone. I do it carefully; I don't want to screw this up. I wave back at her while pressing the mobile against my ear, listening to the hopeful, but almost jeering sound of the dial tone.

"Hello?"

It's not him. A woman. I catch my breath. "Hello.

Is, er, Eric there?"

"Eric? Who's this?" Her voice is gruff. Unfriendly.
Like a dog on a lead barking at me.

"Jessica."

"WHO?"

"Jessica. His daughter."

"His what? Oh . . . *yeah*. Hang on."

It's the way she says "yeah", like I'm something
they've talked about, joked about maybe. Does she
see me as something tragic? "*Oh yeah, that thing!
You know the one.*" I'm pressing the phone harder
against my ear now – it's actually hurting – but I'm
listening, trying to make out muttered words in
the background. Can I hear talking? There sounds
like something, the rise and fall of voices. Are they
talking about me?

"Jess?"

It's him. The voice hasn't changed. Deep, throaty,
like he needs to cough.

"Dad. It's me. I hope you don't mind, but. . ."

"Er, this is not a good time."

"I'm sorry, but. . ."

"You can't just ring up like this. That's not how
it should be. It makes it so awkward." His voice is
small now, almost a whisper.

My mouth is open. I don't know what to say. Hollie is still laughing on the swings, her little legs kicking wildly in the air.

"I'll call you back sometime, yeah?" he says. He sounds so far away. I guess he always was, really.

"When will that be?" I whisper.

"I dunno. Things are tough at the moment. But I'll ring you, yeah?"

I take the phone away from my ear. Press the red button.

Bye, Dad.

No more Dad. I don't need him in my life. I guess I never did. The glitter fairy alarm clock is now upside down in the rubbish bin, where it belongs. A pile of used teabags sits on top of it now, bleeding dark juice on to the worn plastic.

Mum is sitting at the table, looking at the job pages. "What's that you've just thrown away?"

"My alarm clock. It's broken."

"Oh." A brief pause. "*He* got you that, didn't he?"

"Yeah. So?"

She is studying me, a small frown on her face; then she goes back to the paper. "There's nothing in here – never is. I could apply for this cleaning job,

I suppose, at least it would be day work. I wouldn't be so tired all the time, would I? But the money is a little less. . ."

I nod, keeping busy making tea. Opening the cupboards I notice that we have some more stuff in, including cereal. At least this means Mum has been paid. Maybe we could manage. Anything would be better than seeing Mum tired all the time.

"I take it the conversation didn't go well," Mum says, still looking like she's reading.

"He's an idiot." I slam the milk carton on the counter; a small amount spills over the top and down the side. I curse under my breath. "I don't want anything to do with him."

"He's weak. He's never been any good at supporting other people," she sighs. "He's not a bad person though, just a stupid coward."

"If you say so, but it seems to me he's got a new family now." I am trying to find a clean cloth to wipe the spilt milk with, but of course there's nothing. The damp thing in the sink looks like it's breeding a life of its own.

"A new family?" Mum is looking at me again, puzzled. "Really?"

"I saw his girlfriend outside their house with a

baby carrier. There was a nice car outside too," I say. I don't tell her why I was hanging outside their place like some kind of sad weirdo. "I just happened to be passing the other day."

"Well, that's interesting," Mum seems to be drifting off. "I think I need to make some calls of my own, Jess."

She gets up to leave, her face pinched, the paper still clasped in her hand. "Anyway, shouldn't you be getting ready now? Time's ticking on?" She gestures at the clock.

"I'm not going now," I tell her. "I don't feel like it."

"Oh for God's sake, don't tell me you're wimping out now?" She points the paper at me accusingly; it's like a huge extended finger. "Hell, Jess, when are you going to grow a backbone? When are you going to start fighting back?"

She walks out, slamming the door behind her; it makes the clock on the wall shake and almost fall off. I glance at the time. She's right; if I was going I'd be getting ready. The party will be starting in just over half an hour. Twenty past eight makes the clock look like a sad face.

As the minute hand stutters forward, the doorbell goes – shrill and unannounced. Mum yells at me to answer it. We're not expecting anyone, so my stomach drops. It's bound to be someone selling something and I hate having to tell them to go away. Mum says I'm too soft, but I hate seeing their disappointment.

As soon as I open the door, the words hit me — bright and loud.

"You are coming tonight. You have no choice in the matter."

Hannah is standing at my door, hands on her hips, glaring at me. Even more surprising is the sight of the figure lurking behind her.

"Phillip? What on earth are you doing here?"

Phillip blinks hard. "To be honest, Hannah had to twist my arm, literally, to come. As you know, parties aren't really my sort of thing. . ."

"But I told him that you needed our moral support," interrupted Hannah, "so here we are."

I shake my head. "It's nice of you to come but sorry, my mind's made up. I'm not going."

Hannah leans right up close. "Look, I was the first to warn you about Kez before. But you know what, I was wrong. Why should you be the one to hide away? Lyn invited you to his party. It's *his* party – you should be there. He wants you there. So we're here to take you."

"It's like Cinderella," says Phillip dryly, "except I'm *not* your Fairy Godmother."

I can't help laughing at the thought of Phillip in that role.

"Look, can we come in or what?" says Hannah jiggling from one leg to another. "It's freezing out here and I need to use your loo."

Giggling, I lead them in.

"Mum! There's been a change of plan. . ."

We walk to the party together – the three of us. Phillip complains all the way. He hates the cold (it hurts his ears); he hates the dimly lit streets (it hides madmen); he hates the lift in Lyn's tower block (it smells of urine). Hannah has to punch him gently outside Lyn's front door and warn him to at least "try and look normal", before we walk in.

Look normal. I wonder if we do. Hannah does, at least. She's dressed in tight black trousers and a floaty white top that skims beautifully over her flab-less body. Phillip looks awkward in jeans that are slightly too high and a shirt that is just a little too neatly ironed. He looks like a shop dummy, complete with plastic grin. As for me, well, it's just the normal really. Mum assured me I looked beautiful before I left and Hollie even lent me her best plastic bangles to wear. But I know that the jeans I had to dig out are too scruffy. They cling to my bum and bulge at my stomach. I wish I'd gone shopping now and got some new ones. At least Mum's top hides some of my least favourite features and it scoops nicely at the neckline.

I don't think I look like a complete freak.

The door is half open when we arrive so we don't have to knock or anything. Hannah just eases herself in and we follow. The music is already pumping from the back of the flat and there are people everywhere, spilling out into the hall and filling every room we pass.

"This is hell," Phillip hisses in my ear.

I don't answer, but fear is clawing at me. I'm not used to being at parties. My bare arms feel exposed; goosebumps are appearing despite the heat of the flat.

We follow Hannah into the main room which is where the music is coming from. It's a large space and there's no furniture there at all. Just a sofa pushed to the edge of the wall.

"There he is," says Hannah, pointing.

We move towards a group in the corner. Lyn

is leaning against the window sill drinking a beer. He looks gorgeous, completely casual in jeans and a dark T-shirt, but gorgeous all the same. I try not to stare too hard at him.

"Hi," he says, walking over. "Jess! You came!"

I smile back. I notice his mates are grinning at me. I'm not sure if it's friendly or not. The smaller one, Ben/Frodo, seems to be particularly amused by my presence.

"I see you brought your little mates!" says Ben/Frodo, staring intently at Phillip, before shaking his head. He whispers something to the guy next to him and the two of them fall about laughing.

"Take no notice. He's an idiot," Lyn says, looking uncomfortable. "Can I get you anything?"

"No, I'm fine," I say. I become aware of Phillip, standing right behind me. "This is my friend Phillip and that's Hannah over there."

I'm feeling really exposed, like everyone is watching us. Phillip is standing there as wooden as a stick. Hannah has gone off to talk to some Year Tens. This is feeling so awkward.

"Great to meet you," Lyn says, smiling. Phillip stares back at him. He looks like a cat caught in headlights.

"OK. Well I'll leave you to mix then," Lyn says, touching my arm. "We'll catch up later, yeah?"

He walks back to his friends. Ben/Frodo says something else and they all snigger. Alarm bells are flashing in my head and I have no idea how to turn them off.

I turn to Phillip. "Shall we grab a Coke or something?"

"Whatever," he says, shrugging.

We walk out and manage to find the kitchen, which is small and overcrowded. A couple are snogging by the fridge. A girl is sat cross-legged on the floor, texting. I have to manoeuvre past them all to get the Coke bottles.

"Watch it!" the (snogging) girl hisses at me. Her lipstick is smeared all over her face.

"This is fun," mutters Phillip, glaring at the chipped mug that I hand him. He wipes the rim with his hand, frowning.

"It might get better," I say, but in truth I'm feeling the same. I really thought Lyn wanted me here, but now he seems so awkward around me. And why was he sniggering? Is this some kind of joke?

"Jess."

I look up and see Lois standing in the hallway,

blocking my route back through to the living room. My eyes dart around looking to see if Kez is with her, but it looks like she's alone.

"I'm glad you came," she says softly. "I wanted to talk to you."

I find myself backing away from her slightly. The grip on my drink tightens, the tips of my fingers turning white.

"I wanted to have a word," she says.

"OK." I feel my body stiffen. I'm feeling so hot; I can feel the sweat begin to prickle my scalp. My armpits are moist. It's too enclosed here. The walls seem to be pressing against me. "Can we move out there?" I say, gesturing back towards the living room. I need space.

Lois nods. "Sure."

I lead us through the room that has quickly filled up. I try not to look at Lyn, even though my eyes seem to be longing to pull in that direction. I notice that the doors to the balcony have now been released; the thin net curtains are whipping up in the light breeze. I move us towards the opening, immediately welcoming the fresh air that greets us.

Why am I so hot? Everyone else looks so relaxed and cool.

"That's better," I say and smile at Lois, trying to show her the calm "me". The in-control "me".

Lois is frowning a little. She leans in towards me. "I just wanted to. . ."

"Oh, look, there she is!"

Lois spins around; she looks as surprised as me. Beside me, Phillip coughs awkwardly. I don't say anything; I just freeze on the spot. Kez is just standing there, one hand against the wall. She looks gorgeous, head to toe in luscious, skin-tight black. She looks evil. Her eyes are driving through mine, blasts of ice blue. Her lips curl.

"Lois — I see you're catching up with my old mate!" she says loudly, walking towards me. I can see Marnie is behind her, grinning like a nasty sheepdog.

"I just wanted a word," Lois says again.

"Well, you can leave her to me now," Kez says. "This is my problem."

She marches past Lois and comes right up to me. She's never been so close. She looks really mad. Her eyes are bulging and now that I look closely I can see that her make-up has been applied in a rush. Her eyes are smudged and there is a line of foundation around her chin.

"What do you want?" I say.

"I'm here to celebrate with you. Celebrate just what a sad, pathetic little freak you are," she says. She reaches out and pokes her finger into my tummy, her sharp nail hurts but I try not to flinch. "Congratulations – you win the prize for Loser of the Year."

I don't move. Phillip shifts behind me. "Shall we go?" he whispers in my ear. I shake my head. I can't. Not now.

"Look at you – fat, fat, fat. How could you let yourself sink so low?"

"So what?" I say, but my voice is shaking.

She pinches my top between her fingers. "What is this anyway? It's not designer, is it? I bet it's from a tent shop!" Before I know what she's doing, her hand has snaked behind my neck, has reached for the label. "Oh my God, get this, Marnie – she's wearing a maternity top!"

Marnie lets out a whoop of laughter. I think the hole in my heart has just opened up some more, is filling up with fear and shame. I can see everyone looking at me, trying not to laugh.

Really? Is she really wearing a maternity top? How fat must she be?

"So you have to shop in stores for pregnant

women then, Stig? My God, you really have sunk low."

I don't answer. I can see Lois watching and she is shaking her head. Phillip behind me is muttering his disgust, but we are all frozen by Kez's power. And she's not finished yet.

"Do you know what? I'll tell you something, try and help you out a bit, so don't say I never do. Marnie found out from Ben that you were only invited to this party out of pity. That's right –" her face is pressed up right close to mine and I can smell her sour breath "– Lyn felt sorry for you. He wanted you to feel better about yourself so he invited you. How tragic is that? You poor little cow. It's actually pretty sad if you think about it."

She's laughing, right up in my face. Cruel, hard laughs that are cutting right through me.

"That's not true," I whisper, but the tears are rolling down my face now.

"You should just crawl off and die. People like you are better off dead," she hisses, still gripping my top. "You're just a total waste of space."

"Leave me alone," I say, my words barely a whisper. "Don't touch me!" I'm trying to shake her off. I don't want her hands on me. Kez wobbles and gasps, but her grip now tightens. Something in her eyes changes, it's like all of the sparkle has been removed. They look like stone.

"What did you say?" she says.

"I said DON'T TOUCH ME!" I scream now, no longer caring. "You stupid, deaf bitch."

She pushes me, suddenly and with force. She is so strong. All the time she is staring at me with her cold, dead eyes. I fly backwards, out of the patio door and on to the balcony. I'm no longer hot, the cold night air sweeps under my top, across my chest, down my spine. My legs are weak. I want to sink to the floor, but she has me in her claws.

"Please, Kez," I beg. "I'm sorry."

She presses my body against the concrete balustrade. I try and push back but it's like she has the strength of six people. My back is forced against the hard barrier; I can feel myself begin to tip back. I can see the stars, twinkling in the sky. *Such a beautiful night.*

A sneer is plastered across her face. She wants to push me further.

"You're nothing," she hisses. "Nothing. I can shove you now and no one would care. You are worthless."

She pushes me again, my body tips, my neck

almost snapping. My feet are being lifted away from the floor. Someone gasps, I'm not sure who. I can't see, my eyes are blurry. Tears are freely running down my face, a fountain.

"Please, please, please," I beg.

I'm thinking of Hollie. I'm thinking of Mum. Every shred of dignity has been torn away. I imagine falling. Would it be fast and hard? Would I feel any pain? I can hear the beat of time in my head, the rhythm of my own blood rushing to my brain. THUD, THUD, THUD.

"Kez! Let her go!"

I can hear Lyn's voice, somewhere behind. There is movement, shouting. A tug. Suddenly the grip on me is released and I fall to the balcony floor. A fat, wet heap. I scamper on my knees, pushing past anyone standing in my way. I find the doors and pull myself up. I'm shaking, but I keep moving. I can't turn. I can't look at anyone. I hear someone shouting my name, but I don't stop.

I'm running.

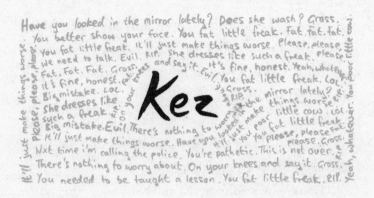

Have you looked in the mirror lately? Does she wash? Gross. You better show your face. You fat little freak. Fat. Fat. Fat. You fat little freak. It'll just make things worse. Please, please, we need to talk. Evil. RIP. She dresses like such a freak. Please, Fat. Fat. Fat. Gross. and say it. It's fine, honest. Yeah, whatever. It's fine, honest. You fat little freak. Loc. Big mistake. LOL. Gross. the mirror lately? She dresses like your RIP. things worse. such a freak. little cow. Lol. Big mistake. Evil. There's nothing to worry your fat little freak. It'll just make things worse. Have you looked just make you poor please, please. Nxt time i'm calling the police. You're pathetic. This is not over. There's nothing to worry about. On your knees and say it. Gross. You needed to be taught a lesson. You fat little freak. RIP.

Kez

I haven't slept. Not much, anyway. I keep thinking about the party later and my mind is whirling. Marnie's spare bed is lumpy; one bump in particular always seems to be there no matter what position I get in. I lay there most of the night staring up at the strange marks on the ceilings, making all sorts of weird pictures out of them – Mr Booth's face in profile, a cat stretching, someone falling.

Marnie wakes me up at ten and we spend most of the morning sitting in her flat. My phone is turned off. I didn't tell Mum where I was last night, she'd work it out for herself. But I know I'll be in big trouble now. Dad will make me pay for this. I'm not even sure I care, I feel so numb.

"You've made it worse for yourself," Marnie says, like she's reading my mind.

"I guess. I just couldn't face it. Not last night anyway."

I'm still hoping the school only spoke to Mum yesterday. I'm still hoping that Dad was too drunk to notice I didn't return home. I'm still hoping all this might go away.

Marnie is preoccupied on her laptop. They are all going on about the party on there. She has been messaging Ben all morning.

"Look, he's pleased I'm coming!" she says, pointing at the latest message. "I knew I was getting there with him!"

Her face is flushed with excitement. She runs into the bathroom and starts searching through her make-up. "I have to look my best tonight. This could be the night we get together."

"Good for you."

"You're pleased for me though?" Her face is accusing. I stand up and move across the room. I keep thinking about what Lyn said last night, about the way he looked at me. I'm sure he hates me now. Hates me and likes *her*.

"Of course I'm pleased. I'm just not feeling too great myself."

Out of her window I can stare over at Tower A. I wonder if Lyn is in there getting excited about tonight. I wonder if he's even thinking of me at all.

"I don't know why you're so upset. Lyn's just a bloke, letting off some steam. Ben told me he doesn't even like Jess."

I turn round. "What?"

"Seriously. He messaged me about it earlier. Lyn just feels sorry for Jess, because of how she looks and stuff. He thinks you're a bit harsh on her. I think that's why he ended it with you."

"Yeah, well. What does he expect? She gets on my nerves," I sniff.

"So what are you going to do then? Sit here feeling sorry for yourself?"

"No. . ."

I think about the message I sent Jess last night. I was raging then, so mad that I could barely contain it, but even now the embers are still burning. How could I let someone like *her* get one over on me? If that happened surely that would mean the end of everything? I'd no longer be Kez; the cool girl at school. I'd be the one who lost out to the fat stig.

You're right," I say, "but I need to get my stuff. Get changed," I tell Marnie.

"Do you want me to come, bit of support?"

I nod. I'm guessing that if Marnie is there,

Dad will ease off me a bit.

No, I'm not guessing. I'm hoping.

"Jeez, Kez, your place is nice!" Marnie says as we walk up the drive.

I pull a face at her. "It's amazing what you can achieve with some hanging baskets and rubbish garden ornaments."

Marnie is wide-eyed. "I'm surprised you want to come back to my place all the time. It must feel like a shoebox compared to this."

I slip the key in the lock and turn the handle carefully, the usual twist of anxiety clutches at my stomach. We step inside. It smells lovely in here, all floral and perfumery. Mum's obviously been cleaning.

As if on cue, she steps out of the lounge, duster in her hand. She looks me up and down, a tiny frown on her face.

"Back then?" she says.

"Obviously." I flap a hand at Marnie. "I stayed over at Marnie's again. Sorry."

"You should tell me. Is it too difficult to tell me?" Her bird-like head is twitching; it always does that when she's nervous or annoyed. I could seriously imagine her pecking birdseed on the front lawn. The bruises on her face are healing. She tries to disguise them with thick foundation, but I can still see the yellow, green tinge there — like an old stain.

"No, sorry," I mumble. I'm aware of Marnie shifting awkwardly behind me. I just want to get away.

"He's out," she says. "Down the pub. He won't be back 'til late."

I nod, relief inching across my skin. "I'm going upstairs to get ready. We're going out later."

Mum looks at me like she wants to say something else, probably about school, but then she just nods. I think she's given up fighting with me.

As we climb the stairs Marnie nudges me. "Look what I smuggled from home."

In her bag is a full bottle of cider. It glistens in the light. I think of Dad and gulping back his cans — the fuel for his anger, my enemy for so long.

"Cool," I say, even though it's far from cool. I hate everything it represents.

But tonight I want to forget. Like he does.

I am so calm walking to Lyn's. My cheeks are stinging in the cold night air and my thoughts are still. Marnie is giggling, stumbling up ahead. She's had far too much to drink, but I held back. I wanted to keep control.

"Oh man, I feel so wrong," she giggles.

I say nothing. It's odd, like I've turned into a machine. Someone has pressed my button and told me what to do. I'm charging forwards. My eyes are focused, blinkered even. I can barely hear anything else.

But I can think about Jess – oh yes, the stig is as clear in my mind as she can be – a sharp focus. I walk with purpose, knowing I will soon be seeing her soppy face again.

"This is going to be wicked. I've got a feeling this will be a night to remember," Marnie says, as she pushes open the heavy doors to Tower A. The sharp scent of its neglect hits me as soon as I step in. It makes me feel a bit sick and have to take shallow breaths to force it back.

We take the lift, there's no way either of us could cope with the stairs in our silly heels. Three boys I don't recognize are already waiting by the doors; pressing the button repeatedly like it would it make it come any faster. Idiots.

"Are you going to the party?" one of them asks.

He looks a lot older than us, eighteen maybe, with a shaven head and cool hazel eyes. I don't recognize him from school, so I assume he's from the Estate.

"Yeah, are you?" says Marnie. She walks up closer to them. She's even more confident tonight. I hang back, watching as she leans against the wall, chatting to them. There's nothing that fazes her. I find it odd how she can be so confident with anyone, even complete strangers. Does she ever feel insecure?

I think of Lyn. I think of his beautiful, dark eyes, his full lips. The way he used to stroke my face. I can't even remember how I got into this mess.

Oh yes, her. . .

"C'mon, Kez. What are you doing?" Marnie shouts over.

The boys are laughing. I look and see the lift has arrived; reluctantly I join them.

"You've got a face on you," Marnie says, as we squeeze into the lift. It's a tight fit and it smells even worse in here, my throat is tightening even more. There might as well be a hand around it, gripping me.

"I just want to get there," I say.

I just want to get to HER!

"You look like you mean business," says the guy

with the shaven head. He's looking at me intently. I just glare back. I don't want to talk. I want this all to be over with.

The doors slide open and a gust of stale air blasts in. The boys tumble out first, loud and laughing. We let them go ahead. Marnie pulls on my arm. We step out into the corridor. I can hear music already, pumping from the opposite end.

"Do I look all right?" she says, her face scrunched up in concern.

"You're fine," I say, although I'm probably not in the best mood to judge. I'm feeling heavy, like a huge weight is resting upon me.

"C'mon then." She grabs my hand and leads me in.

The door to Lyn's flat is standing open; the music is much louder now. I freeze for a second, remembering being here yesterday. My heart seems to be beating extra hard, in time to the beat of the bass.

"Are you OK?" Marnie asks.

"Yeah, fine," I snap, pushing past her.

At first it's hard to make out who's who in the shapes of the crowd in the hallway. It's dimly lit in there and so hot. I move awkwardly, trying to find someone I recognize. First, I see Lois, standing with her back to me, she's talking to someone. Then, I realize who. A rush of adrenaline hits me; I push myself over to them. I can feel the power surge through me, like electricity.

I watch as Lois spins round. A haze of faces are staring straight at me, but I can't work them out. My head, my whole body is buzzing with energy.

I say something – angry, bitter words. I can't remember what, my brain is fuzzy. I watch as Lois backs away. She hates me when I'm like this; I know she'll want to get away from me. I find myself walking towards Jess. She's standing there like a useless lump. I want to grab her – in my unsteady shoes I almost lean on her – but I manage to hold back.

I reach towards her instead. My finger lands in the folds of her belly, soft like a sponge cake. I find myself prodding it again and again, so soft. More words are floating out of my mouth, but they feel fat and heavy. I have no control. I'm a clockwork toy; all wound up and primed to spill my hatred. I know I'm hurting her, each word is having impact.

I grab at her top. It's pretty. Madly, she looks quite nice in it. My clumsy fingers find the label; I see that it's a maternity top. She must be having a laugh, surely?

"Oh my God, get this, Marnie, she's wearing a maternity top!" I shout.

That's funny isn't it? I mean, who goes around wearing a top for pregnant women. Jess's face seems to be changing. Her jaw is dropping. I'm going to make her cry.

Good.

So I tell her. I tell her Lyn only invited her out of pity, that he felt sorry for her. I can hear the anger in my words, I know exactly what effect they are having but I keep on slamming them at her. It's about time the poor deluded cow heard the truth.

You can't have Lyn! He'd never be interested in you. He's mine.

I'm wobbling now, running out of words, but I'm really getting to her. I can see it. Jess is standing there, not moving. She is as pale as a ghost. I only see it for a flicker, but it's enough, for that briefest second my mum is in front of me – my pathetic, weak, cowardly mum.

"Please, I'll be good from now on, I promise, just don't hurt me again. . ."

I tell Jess she's better off dead. Because cowards

are, aren't they? Who wants to be like that? I can see I've shocked her. Her eyes are wide. Then suddenly her mouth flies opens.

"I said DON'T TOUCH ME!" she screams, right in my face. "You stupid, deaf bitch."

Spit hits my chin. I just snap. How dare she say that to me! Red rage. Heat in my face. Pure venom. I push her. I have strength that I never knew was there, and she seems as light as a doll. Her face is tipped towards me, her mouth open, gaping wide. Disgusting.

I feel the cold air as we rush out on to the balcony, my head immediately seems lighter. I want to get her away from me. She disgusts me. She is everything I don't want to be. I force her up against the hard wall. I press hard. I watch as she tips a little, a rush of something floods me. I can't describe it – is it energy? A thrill? Evil?

I'm saying things, but all sounds are muffled. All I can concentrate on is her face. Her round, scared, stupid face.

I can push her over.

I will push her over.

She will land with a thud. She will leave a crater in the ground. She will be gone for ever.

She is begging me. Her mouth working overtime. "Please, please, please." Whispers in the wind.

I shove her again, just a bit. I see the terror, sheer panic in her eyes. My grip is loosening, I'm going to let go.

"Kez! No!"

Lyn is behind me. Where did he come from? He pulls me back roughly, strong arms round my waist. I gasp. I still have hold of her. She falls to the balcony floor.

I could've pushed her over.

I could've.

I wanted to.

I'm flung against a wall. People are moving, shouting. The cloud in my head is shifting. I can see people running towards the front door, calling after Jess. Screaming at her to come back. I have an urge to laugh. It's all so mad, so crazy.

I could've done it. I wanted to. . .

I squint and see Lyn is there, shoving his way to the front of the crowd. I go to call to him, but someone pulls on my arm.

"What the hell did you just do?"

Lois forces herself in front of me. Her face is flushed red.

"What? I was just messing around," I say, but the lie feels wrong. "You've been just as bad."

This throws her for a second; she bites her lip, then shakes her head softly. "No, don't pin this one on me, Kez. You were bang out of order. You just laid into her. What you said — it was evil. And out there — you nearly pushed her over the edge!"

"Evil!" I snort. Like she knows what evil is! Perfect little Lois.

"Yes, bloody evil. What have you become?"

I pull myself up straighter, trying hard to regain some control. I just wish I didn't feel so sick. "I wasn't going to push her," I say, but I know I sound unconvincing. I keep looking at my hands. I know what I nearly did.

"God knows what effect that will have on her. She's been looking bad for weeks, I've been so worried. I told you this might happen. I warned you to stop."

"Oh yeah!" I say. "Says you! You were the one having a go at her when I walked in."

"Oh my God!" Lois is almost laughing now. "How could you get this so wrong? I wanted to see if she was OK. I've been feeling so guilty for what we've been putting her through. What you and Marnie have been putting her through. . ."

Her words hang in the air.

"It was just a bit of a laugh," I mutter. My head is starting to throb now. I can see people are coming back into the flat. Lyn is there, he is staring straight at me. Others are staring too. Shaking their heads. They all hate me.

"It's not a laugh though, is it? It's nasty. You're just doing what your little mate tells you. You do know this is exactly what Marnie wanted to happen?" Lois says, her voice rising now.

"What?" I can't get a grip on all this and my eyes can't leave Lyn. He's moving towards me.

"Marnie enjoys winding you up and watching you attack. You're like a toy to her. But when the crap hits the fan, where is she?"

I glance behind, I assumed she would be in the crowd behind me, but there is no sign.

"She went off with Ben a few minutes ago," says Lois, softly. "She stopped being interested as soon as Jess ran away. All she wants is the drama, Kez. She's no friend at all. Does she even notice what's going on in your house?"

"What?" I hiss.

"Do you think I'm stupid? I've seen your Mum's bruises. Is that what you are now, Kez. A bully like your dad?"

I freeze. Lois just stares at me, nodding. She knows.

"I'm not," I whisper, but the words are lame and barely register. I can't even think straight. I'm shaking. I look at my hands again and back up. Who am I? Lyn is standing right in front of me now; I barely recognize him. His face is like granite. He looks hard and cool.

"You're a complete bitch," he says.

"I'm sorry." I reach over, longing to touch his face, tell him I'm not really like this. Tears are pricking my eyes, teasing me.

"Why did you do it?" he says, backing away from me. "I just don't get it. You could've killed her. And now she's gone, disappeared, thanks to you."

"Marnie said you weren't interested in her, that you felt sorry for her. She deserved to know the truth." I think I'm slurring now. They both seem to be looking at me in disgust.

"And she deserved to die too, did she?" Lois barks at me. "That's what you told her."

"I didn't say that. . ." I whisper. "Did I?"

Words. Words. Words. What did I say? It was only words, letters linked together. I can't even remember. But I could've hurt her badly. I almost did. . .

"I never felt sorry for her. Ben and Marnie are just stirring and you are a gullible idiot for falling for it."

"So you do like her?" I say, resentment bubbling.

"Yeah, maybe I do. She's a better person than you'll ever be," he says. "You're jealous, Kez. A jealous, little bully. You're pathetic."

I back away. I can't stand looking at him. Everything feels unreal. Perhaps I'll wake up in minute, maybe this whole week has just been a sick dream.

I want Marnie. I need to leave. I run into the living room. There are people everywhere, I hate them all. I barge them out of my way. I push. I shove.

Marnie is sat on Ben's lap on the sofa. They are kissing. The girl got her man.

"Maz, I need to leave," I say, touching her arm.

She pulls herself away. "No, Kez, I'm not leaving."

I am thinking of Lyn in the hallway. I'm thinking of Jess running away from me. I'm thinking of Jess's face as she looked up at me, begging. I'm thinking about Dad waiting for me, in our clean, cold house.

"But I need you," I plead. "It's all gone wrong."

"Tough, sort it yourself," she says and goes back to Ben.

Finally, I can see.

You poor little cow. She offends my eyes. Big mistake. On your knees and say it. This is not over. Please, please, please. Have you looked in the mirror lately? There's nothing to worry. RIP fat. face. RIP. This is not over. We need to talk. LOL. Evil. Gross. LOL. Does she wash? Evil. Does she wash? Evil. This is not over. We need to talk. LOL. This is not over. Fat. Poor little cow. You needed to talk. LOL. please, please. be taught a please. Evil. Gross. lesson. It's fine, You're pathetic. Fat. worry about the police. On your knees and honest. Next time I'm calling the police. say it. Gross and RIP. Evil. There's nothing you fat little freak. Fat. Fat. RIP. fat. Big mistake. Gross. Yeah, whatever. You needed to be taught a lesson. It'll just make things wo... Have you looked in the mirror lately? It's fine, honest. RIP. She dresses like such a freak.

Jess

I tell Phillip and Hannah to go back to the party. I don't want them. I don't want anyone around me. I want to be alone. They don't listen, of course – they never do.

We walk home in near silence. They keep saying stuff, but I don't answer, everything has shut down. I feel numb and calm, far too calm.

Outside my house Hannah hugs me. Her fingers grip my skin.

"You will be OK, won't you?" she says.

I smile at her. A weak, thin smile, but it's all I have.

I watch and wave as they leave me at my front door. As soon as they've gone I let myself in.

I have things to do.

221

Have you looked in the mirror lately? Does she wash? Gross. . You better show your face. You fat little freak. Fat. Fat. Fat. you fat little freak. It'll just make things worse. Please, please, we need to talk. Evil. RIP. She dresses like such a freak. Please, Fat. Fat. Fat. Gross. and say it. Evil. It's fine, honest. Yeah, whatever It's fine, honest. You fat little freak. Lol. Big mistake. LoL. Gross. She dresses like RIP. the mirror lately? such a freak. things worse Big mistake. Evil. There's nothing to worry fat little freak. It'll just make things worse. Have you look Kill you poor you please, please Nxt time I'm calling the police. You're pathetic. This is not over. please. Gross. There's nothing to worry about. On your knees and say it. Gross. You needed to be taught a lesson. You fat little freak. RIP.

Kez

I've never been scared to be on my own before, but tonight I am. It's late. I don't like it.

I manage to grab a bus outside Lyn's and sit at the back, huddled away. There's hardly anyone else there. An old man in a hat, an African lady singing softly under her breath, a woman dressed in red reading a battered book.

Maybe I could stay on this bus, just carry on going. Where would I end up? Where would I go next? Could I cope alone?

I sit picking at the material on the seat, making a small hole. I can stick my finger right in.

I'm good at this. I'm good at destroying things.

I am my dad.

Kez Walker: I've realized now, what I am. I'm not a good person. I can't carry on like this. Trouble is, I don't know how to stop, but *Jessica Pearson* never deserved this.

Just now.

Like   **Comment**   **Share**

0 Comments

Sunday

You poor little cow. She offends my eyes. Big mistake. On your knees and say it. This is not over. Please, please, please face. RIP. Have you looked in the mirror lately? There's nothing to worry. RIP fat. This is not over. We need to talk. LOL. Evil. Gross. LOL. Does she wash? Evil. Does she Evil. wash? This is not over. Fat. Poor little cow. We need to talk. LOL. please, please, You needed to please. Evil. Gross. be taught a lesson. It's fine, You're pathetic. Fat. worry about the police. honest. Nxt time I'm calling On your knees and you fat little freak. Say it. Gross and RIP. Evil. There's nothing to Big mistake. Gross. Fat. Fat. Fat. You needed to be taught a lesson. It'll just make things wor— Have you looked in the mirror lately? It's fine, honest. RIP. She dresses like such a freak. We need to talk. Gross. LOL. whether she washes or not. Yeah, whatever.

Hollie has had a bad dream, really nasty. She sits up, screaming, sweating, thrashing her legs. Mum is home and has to come in to try and calm her down, but Hollie is still trapped. She points at the wall, tells us that there is something there. Her eyes can't see us. Our words can't soothe her. In the end she falls back on to her tangled sheets, muttering under her breath, her eyes still fluttering under her now closed lids.

"It's a night terror," Mum whispers, "she must be worrying about something."

"Worrying? She's only five."

"Kids pick up on things." Mum glances at me. "You look awful, have you slept at all?"

I instinctively look over at my alarm clock, but of course it's gone. "What time is it?"

"Nearly seven. I've not been up long myself,"

227

Mum touches my arm. "Come into the kitchen, I've got something to tell you."

I pick up my dressing gown and we walk through the dark hall, Mum flicks on a light and we both blink hard. I sit myself down at the table; I am sick with tiredness, I've spent the last few hours remembering the previous evening. I keep thinking about that sky, tipping backwards. The fear of actually falling. Everything's changed now.

Mum fiddles around by the sink. "Let's have a hot chocolate. You used to love those when you were little."

I nod. "OK."

I watch as she scoops powder into the cup, mixes it into the cold milk. She's doing it all wrong, it'll go all lumpy now.

"I'm not going to do night shifts any more," Mum says, clanking the spoon against the china. "It's not fair on any of us. I've managed to swap with Debs, she needs the extra money. I'll be doing morning work now, cleaning some private houses over by the Gearton Estate."

"That's great," I say. "But don't we need the money?"

"That's the thing. I spoke to your dad last night. Well, spoke isn't really the right word. . . That man has been giving us the runaround for too long. He'd told me he was broke, told me that he was so ill he couldn't get out of bed most days. But, if he's well enough to father another child. . ."

"What did he say?"

"Not much. Once I threatened him with legal action he agreed to more regular payments, it should help a bit." She pauses, spoon in mid-air. "I did mention you too, Jess, but . . . I don't know . . . he just hasn't got a clue."

"What do you mean?"

"I mean, he's no good with kids, being a dad. That's partly why he left here in the first place. I pity the poor little mite that he's bringing up now. Sometimes you just have to accept that people don't always make good parents."

"I guess."

"He might change," she adds, her voice laced with doubt.

We remain in silence, watching the mugs warm in the microwave. The only sound is the soft whir of the machine. I sit and wonder about Hollie. What was it she saw crawling up the walls? Would it be better if she could tell us what was scaring her? The microwave beeps.

"I've written something, Mum," I say suddenly.

"Eh?" Mum places the hot chocolate in front of me, steaming hot. "What's that?"

I reach in the pocket of my dressing gown and pull out the piece of paper. It's carefully folded up.

"It's exactly what's been going on, all listed down. I want you to do something now. I want it to stop."

She reads it slowly, her face paling slightly. "My God, she did this to you? This is awful. We should call the police. How long has Kez been like this with you? I never knew it was so bad."

I can feel something inside me shift. I don't have to do this on my own any longer. I nod, I feel lighter somehow. Calmer.

"Not any more," Mum whispers. "Not any more."

It's ten o'clock, I don't want to go online at all, I want to go back to bed, but Mum tells me to. She says I need to block Kez and her lot, that way I won't get to see all the nasty comments they keep making. So I log on. Straight away I see that I've been tagged in an update by Kez. My heart sinks. Surely she's done enough? But I make myself click on it.

You can't get to me, Kez. Not now. Not again.

I read her message once and then again. It's cold and bleak and it's wrong.

KEZ: I've realized now, what I am. I'm not a good person. I can't carry on like this. Trouble is, I don't know how to stop, but *Jessica Pearson* never deserved this.

Something just clicks into place. A bad feeling swoops through me.

I quickly search for the only person that might be able to help.

Thankfully, he's there. He's waiting.

Lyn.

"Are you sure this is the right thing to do?" I ask him.

"I guess. She's not answering her phone. We need to check she's OK, don't we?"

We're standing outside Kez's house. It's beautiful, like the places you see on TV dramas, all neat and tidy and perfectly designed.

"I've not actually been inside before, she always kept me away," Lyn says, squinting up at the netted windows. "But I walked past once. She didn't know. I just wanted to see what it was like."

"It's lovely, isn't it?"

"You wonder why she wants to hang around the Estate all the time. Why is she always hiding away from here?"

I walk over to the front door and ring the bell. It's a nice, friendly chime. Welcoming. We both stand back and wait. Lyn stuffs his hands in his pockets and rocks back on his heels. He looks so awkward, out of place. Maybe that's why Kez kept him away? Is it wrong that I want to touch him? But then I remember what Kez told me and I step away.

He was never interested.

The door opens slowly and a tiny, thin woman peers round. She has short dark hair and an angular, sharp-looking face. I notice she has a large bruise on her cheek and some yellowing under her eye, like a nicotine stain. She's trying to keep her head turned away so we can't see it, I'm sure of it. I can tell she's Kez's mum though from the bright blue eyes.

"Hi," I say. "Is Kez in?"

She rolls her eyes. "Kez does as she pleases. She disappeared out about half an hour ago. She was home late last night and then was up with the birds."

"Oh." I hesitate before asking. "Did she seem OK?"

"I didn't see her, just heard the front door slam."

She blinks rapidly a few times. "Look, is there a problem? I must admit it's odd for her to be up so early. Is she OK?"

Lyn steps forwards. "Sorry to burst in on you like this, we're just a bit worried about her. Did she leave a note or anything? Say what time she'd be back?"

Kez's mum shakes her head. "Oh, you better come in. I'll go and check."

We step into the hallway. It's huge and shiny, every area seems freshly polished. I'm scared to step too far in case I mark anything. Kez's mum gestures for us to wait there, while she dashes back upstairs.

"Who's that?"

A voice booms from a room above. I see Kez's mum freeze briefly on the stair and then she calls up. "It's nothing, love, just friends of Keren's."

"Tell them to go, then; Keren won't be allowed friends round here, little cow."

I turn to Lyn and he pulls a face at me, this is suddenly very uncomfortable. I hear the thud of footsteps, the slam of a door and then a man appears at the top of the stairs. He is large and red faced, a blue dressing gown pulled tight around his large middle.

"I'm Keren's dad," he booms. "Why are you here?"

"We're just checking she's OK," Lyn says calmly.

"And why wouldn't she be OK?" His voice is like ice, hurtling towards us. "Surely I should know?"

"It's probably nothing. . ." I start to say, but am interrupted by a piercing scream coming from another room. All our heads turn.

Kez's mum staggers out towards us. She seems almost unable to hold herself upright. "You did this!" she screams at her husband. She runs towards him and hits him hard on the arm.

He seems genuinely shocked. "I did what?"

"This!" she yells and thrusts a letter into his hand.

Everything goes a bit crazy. Kez's mum is sobbing in the living room; her dad starts pacing up and down, muttering under his breath. He looks like he's in a trance. Then he opens the door that leads to the patio and stands there smoking a cigarette.

"I want you OUT!" she keeps screaming at him, but he's not listening. He doesn't even answer. His smoke is curling into the room and he doesn't seem to care. He looks lost.

Lyn has the note and is checking it again. "It says if we're reading this, she's succeeded. That means she has something planned. We have to act fast."

"But what? What is she planning?" Kez's mum sobs.

I keep thinking of her writing that note, putting down those words. I never knew how bad she was feeling. How could this be the same Kez I'd feared for so long?

"I'll try Marnie," Lyn says. "She might know something." He leaves the room with his phone clasped in his hand, shooting me a concerned look.

"I'm calling the police," Kez's mum says. "We can't leave it any longer."

I sit and listen to her voice cracking over the phone; she is barely able to provide the details. She makes weird choking noises in her throat. I want to hug her, but her body is stiff and turned away from me. She puts down the phone and visibly shudders, before walking to the other side of the room. She stands by the patio doors and stares out, like she could find Kez out there.

"I never knew she felt like this," Kez's dad mutters. I don't think he is talking to us. He is pacing the room again, staring straight ahead like a zombie. "She never seemed depressed or anything."

"No. . ." I reply. Who knew?

Lyn comes back into the room. Kez's mum turns and looks at him hopefully, big wide eyes. "No," he says. "Marnie was still in bed. She's not heard from Kez."

And I bet she didn't even care. . .

Lyn sits down next to me on the sofa. His face looks sunken. "I said some horrible things to her," he whispers. "But after what she did to you. . ."

I shrug. "I'm OK."

"But she just went for you on the balcony. And she said those awful things." He looks so pale, sick even. "That stuff about me was crap, Jess. I never felt sorry for you. I really, really like you."

A warm feeling. I can't stop it.

"Really?" I say.

He nods, a small smile is settling on his lips.

Kez's mum jumps up as the doorbell goes. "That was quick," she says, running across the room, slamming the door behind her. We hear muffled talking in the hallway. I stare around the large living room, feeling so uncomfortable. I know I shouldn't even be here. She didn't even like me.

Suddenly, my eyes fall on a painting above the fireplace. It's really pretty, despite being quite crude. Lots of poppies in a large field. A scrawl of a name is etched in the far corner.

I turn to Kez's dad. "Did Kez paint that?" I ask.

He stops pacing and looks up at the picture. "Yes, she did. She loves painting. She always did her favourite places. That was a field we saw on holiday in Wales." He keeps staring at it, like he's hypnotized.

Suddenly, a thought comes to me; I'm not sure why I didn't think of it before.

"There's somewhere I need to go," I whisper to Lyn. "I think I might know where Kez is."

Lyn turns to me, alarmed. "Tell the police then? Or at least let me come with you."

"But I might be wrong. It's a long shot." I squeeze his hand, pleading. "Please just cover for me. Tell them I've nipped home or something. I won't be long, promise."

He nods softly. Kez's dad is still in a trance, he doesn't notice as I slip out of the open patio door.

The cool morning air greets me as I walk out of the side gate. And then I run.

I just pray I've got this right.

Is she here? Please, please be here. . .

The bridge is such a weird, haunting place, both ugly and beautiful at the same time and totally overgrown now. An empty shell set in wild flowers and weeds, tall above the ravine that was once the deep railway cutting. Kez saw the beauty and that's why she painted it. It just took seeing another one of her paintings for me to remember.

One of her favourite places. . .

She is standing on the bridge; I can see this as soon as I round the corner. The bridge itself is like a downturned mouth, its teeth rotted away. Where there should be bars, there are just great big gaps and she is standing in one of these. It's like she's looking out of a huge, jagged window. All that's keeping her there is one hand, holding on to the thin rail that once held everything in place.

She only has to dip her head. She only has to let go and she would fall through that gap, like a small, wingless bird.

I approach her carefully, picking my way through brambles, decaying crisp packets, tangled up carrier bags. By the time I reach the foot of the stairs, my legs are already criss-crossed in scratches and marks. Red-and-white tape still binds the metal at the base. A flattened barrier is a reminder that we shouldn't be here – this place is unsafe.

There were whispered rumours that they were going to smash this thing down. Build offices instead with huge glass windows. But then the recession came and I think the bridge was forgotten, along with so many things. Nobody comes here anyway. Who'd want to? It's a death trap.

A perfect place to die.

I hadn't realized how bad it had become though. It has slowly been rotting away in the background, while we just carried on. So many things are left, forgotten about.

I have to tread on the tape and pick my way up the steps carefully. The metal is so corroded and rusty, there are parts where it's worn through completely. I'm scared I'll trap my foot on a broken bit. I'm virtually on tip-toe. She still hasn't noticed me though. I'm moving as slow as I can, almost too scared to breathe, my eyes fixed on her static, upright body.

Please don't jump. Please don't jump. Please. . .

My mind wanders for a moment. Why do I even care? Why the hell should I help her after all she's done? I pause and take a long, shaky breath. An image of Hollie flashes in my mind; her soft face, her kind eyes. If she was here, she'd be tugging my arm, dragging me along.

"You have to help, Jess. You have to do the right thing."

I blink hard and keep moving.

I quickly reach the top. What now? I'm hardly

an expert in these things. I'm even more scared that the bridge will collapse under my weight.

I take a step. The bridge creaks. My breath leaves me in a sudden burst, a whoosh of air.

Kez's head spins round, she sees me and her eyes widen. Mascara streaks her face in dark stripes.

"Go away!" she screams. "Go away, or I swear I'll jump!"

She tips her body slightly, still gripping the bar. I swear the whole bridge shakes with the movement. I think I'm going to be sick.

"Please, Kez, stay there. I won't come any closer."

"I will do it. I will!"

I sit myself on the floor. "See. I'm not moving. Please just step back."

It's hard down here, rough. My leg grazes the metal. I see her hesitate, her shoulders slacken.

"Please, Kez, just listen to what I have to say."

She's just standing there, a frozen statue. The breeze lifts the curl of her hair and it drifts up slightly, like smoke.

"Surely this isn't want you want," I say. "Do you really want to end it all?"

"Yes. . ." Her voice is a breath. I barely recognize it.

"But is it your life you want to end? Or just the

crap? Do you want to die, or do you just want things to be different?"

Her arms wobble slightly. I'm fixated on her hands, her tiny hands. The hands that nearly pushed me over just hours before. *Please don't let that grip loosen...*

"I want things to be different too, you know. And they can be. It's not too late. It never is," I plead.

She doesn't answer, but I can see a change in her stance, a softening. It's almost as if she's moving towards me, even though she hasn't shifted an inch.

"I remembered your painting at school. It made me think you might be here," I say. "I love your paintings."

I pull myself up and slowly walk towards her. Each creak makes me flinch, but I'm committed now. I keep my eyes glued on her back, praying that she stays just there and doesn't move.

That's it... Keep still... Just stay there, please, just stay there...

"But why, Kez?" I continue. "What's so special about this bridge?"

"Dad used to bring me here," she says flatly. "We used to make camps underneath. It was good then, you know? When I was really little. Happy. I just can't seem to remember those times now. Sometimes coming here brings it back to me a little bit."

"But you don't want to jump, do you," I say. It's not a question. I just pray I've read this right. I sit down again now, right beside her. Her feet are just inches away from my legs. I can smell her perfume. Sweet, heady.

You can't go now. I'm here, right here. Stay with me!

"I wanted to. But then I got here and I remembered again. . . Oh, I don't know. I'm so pathetic I can't even do this properly." She starts to sob softly. "Am I such a bad person?"

"No. But you did a bad thing."

She nods.

"You don't even hate me, do you?" I say.

"No." She turns to face me. "You just annoy the hell out of me, you remind me so much of her – of my mum. Just putting up with the abuse day after day, rolling over like a dog. It made me look down on you, I guess. I was wrong."

"But why the fat comments? Why make it so personal?"

"It was just something to latch on to," she says. "To be honest it could've been anything. It was just a thing to use against you. I'm sorry. I don't know why I snapped. It was awful, to think I nearly. . ." she gasps.

242

"But you didn't," I say.

I look up at her. Most of the make-up washed away, no Marnie, no power. This is the real Kez.

"I did an awful thing," she cries.

"It's OK," I say.

"I'm a monster."

"No. You're not."

"I'm like him."

"You're Kez. You're whoever you want to be."

"Do you think my mum will ever leave him?" she asks suddenly.

I think of the bruise on her mum's face, of the shouting when I first arrived. "I don't know," I say, "maybe?"

She laughs softly. "At least you're honest."

"We have more in common than you think," I tell her. "I'm getting used to having a rubbish dad."

"Really?"

"Yeah. It's not easy, but I've accepted that he's probably not going to be around. That's fine. I've got a great mum."

"You're stronger than I realized," Kez says.

"Not really. I have wobbles too." I think of that last phone call to Dad and I still feel a little shiver inside me. "But it's getting easier."

"I don't think I can face going home," she whispers.

"But where else can you go?" I say. "You can't keep running. Or hiding."

"How do you keep going when everyone's on your case?" she asks. "Seriously? I used to think you were so weak, but now I see it's me that's the coward. I can't face anything."

"I don't have the magic answers. I just take each day as it comes." My fingers are running across the rough metal, sharp, almost cutting into me. It's so high up here. I squeeze myself right next to Kez, into the gap in the slats. I push my legs through. It feels nicer somehow, more free. Kez looks down, watching. Then very slowly she pulls herself down beside me. She's crouching, like she's a bit unsure where to put herself.

"Wouldn't you prefer it if I wasn't around?" she asks, her voice sounding so thin.

"Not like this." I sigh. "I just wanted it to stop. All the hassle, all the name calling – that's all."

"It will now," she whispers. "It has to."

"What about Marnie?"

"I don't know about her now. Being with her was fun, she took my mind off so much stuff, but . . . I don't know. I'm not sure she was ever my friend."

I nod. "I guess I can deal with her anyway."

"I really think Lyn likes you," she says. "I guess I need to face the fact he was never that into me. I think he fancies something about you."

"Maybe he just goes for fatties!"

She looks over at me, shocked. But then she sees I'm laughing. A small smile creeps across her face.

"Maybe he does," she says.

Kez moves down and pushes her legs in the gap beside me so that we are wedged up closer, legs hanging free. There is still a gap between us, a few inches. I think there always will be.

"That's better," she says.

I look down at the tracks, watching our legs swinging above the overgrown scrub and rocks below us. Tiny flower buds are shooting up, nestled among the weeds and moss. Long green vines climb up the rusty legs of the bridge, bright and vibrant.

I think it might be OK now.

I think.

Have you looked in the mirror lately? Does she wash? Gross. . You better show your face. You fat little freak. Fat. fat. fat. you fat little freak. It'll just make things worse. Please, please we need to talk. Evil. RIP. She dresses like such a freak. Please Fat. Fat. Fat. Gross and say it. It's fine, honest. Yeah, whatever it's fine, honest. Big mistake. LOL. She dresses like such a freak Big mistake. Evil. There's nothing to worry in the mirror lately? It'll just make things worse. Have you looked things worse Nxt time i'm calling the police. You're pathetic. This is not over. There's nothing to worry about. On your knees and say it. Gross. You needed to be taught a lesson. You fat little freak. RIP.

Kez

Sometimes in the darkness you begin to see so clearly. Because of this I do know that:

    a) Bullies are scum.

    b) Families should be there when you need them.

    c) I was weak. I thought I deserved this.

But I also realize that:

    d) Bullies can change.

    e) Families get it wrong.

    f) Hurting isn't a weakness. The strength comes
       from moving on.

I hope one day I can tell Jess just how sorry I really am.

But, until that day comes, I'll keep moving out of the darkness and back into the light.

Perhaps I have done something right for once.

I'm changing. I'm trying.

A new week is beginning.

Acknowledgements

A huge thanks to the wonderful team at Scholastic for your support, and to Zoë, Gen and Emily, my wonderful editors.

I would love to thank Stephanie at Curtis Brown for plucking me from her tumbling slush pile and being an amazing agent.

Thanks to Tom for making me smile, reading my very rough drafts and believing in me throughout.

Thanks to my family for their constant love and encouragement, and to my wonderful friends, who know who they are.

And thanks to Mr Anthony, my primary school teacher, who inspired me to write.

As a young girl, Eve spent her time telling stories to the birds at the bottom of the garden. Then she learnt to write and a new world opened up. She hasn't stopped since.

Following university, she began a career in business, but found herself spending more time gazing out of the window, dreaming of being a writer. Eventually she left her seventh-floor office to begin a career in pastoral support, and later child protection, in a large local secondary school. The teenagers she works with challenge the way she thinks and inspire her on a daily basis.

Seven Days developed from the idea that every story has two sides. Bullies can also be victims. Eve knew she wanted to write contemporary fiction with a gritty edge. Fiction that young people could relate to. She hopes she has done OK.

Eve lives in West Sussex with her husband, two children and a demented cat, Ziggy. She still tells stories to the birds in the garden – but only when no one is looking.